SILKEN ROAD

SILKEN ROAD

A QUEST IN INTRIGUE, WAR, AND ROMANCE

K. K. SULLIVAN

FlimFlam Enterprises

Springfield, Nebraska

FlimFlam
Enterprises

www.FlimFlamEnterprises.com
Paperback ISBN: 978-1-7360739-0-2
Library of Congress Cataloging data on file with the publisher.

Designed and produced by Concierge Marketing Book Publishing Services.

Printed in the United States of America.

10 9 8 7 6 5 4 3 2 1

To the brave women who put themselves in harm's way to keep us safe and secure.

CHAPTER 1 - MOM1

The sharp rap of knuckles against wood echoed through the house.

"Someone get the door," Maxine called from the kitchen.

Rita wiped her hands on a dishrag and hustled over. She swung the door open and blinked in surprise.

"Oh, Mom! It's you?" she exclaimed.

"Who were you expectin', Saint Nicholas?" snapped Mary Magdalene-Waugh Sullivan, born in Ireland in 1893, standing all of five foot six with the stance of a woman who brooked no nonsense.

"Where's Shirley?" Ma demanded, stepping inside without waiting for an invitation.

"Right here, Ma," Shirley piped up from the stairwell.

"And where's that mutt beag of yours?" Ma asked, eyes narrowing.

Shirley leaned against the banister, lips quirking. "Pawing her way to Charlottesville on North US29, then planning a swim in the Potomac."

"*Pingin-eagnaí agus punt-baosrach!*" Ma snapped, shaking her head. "Pennywise and pound-foolish," she muttered. "Now, young lady, who put that smart mouth on you? Your father? One of your three lovely sisters? Or one of your six darling brothers?"

"Seven brothers, Ma. You're forgetting one," Shirley corrected, grinning.

Ma's hand flew to her hip. "Of all people, don't you be countin' for me, girl. I know my own brood. Leonard's off doin' Army work. He's not here."

"Yes, he is," Shirley countered, tipping her chin toward the hall. "Right behind you. And he's the one who told me to say it—in his cockamamie W.C. Fields imitation."

Ma turned slowly, her eyes narrowing as she locked onto Leonard. Her face flushed, and out came the Celtic shotgun blast: "*Gabh bhur teanga beagán feoirling mé toilím ní rabhadh tú arís!*"

Doc leaned toward Helen, whispering, "That's not a good thing, is it?"

Helen winced. "Oh no. It's worse than bad. She just told him, 'Hold your tongue, little farthing. I shall not warn you again.'"

"Sneakin' up on your poor old mother instead of facin' her like a man," Ma growled. "I ought to send you outside to cut a switch—no supper for you!"

Leonard laughed and stepped forward. "Ah, come here, Ma. You know you'd miss yellin' at me if I didn't keep you on your toes." He kissed her cheek, and her scowl softened... slightly.

But her sharp gaze shifted to Doc. "So, Leonard, who's this woman?" she demanded, jabbing a finger toward her. "Leo, I thought you were datin' Dolores? Or was it Harold? Wasn't he seein' Dolores? And Raymond—weren't you sweet on that Betty McGuire girl? Jack, where's Harriet tonight? Robert, you've got a date with Denita tomorrow, don't you? And Richard—you're too young for girls."

Her eyes swept back to Doc. "So, no takers? No secrets? Then who does the *Coill nimfeach* belong to?"

"Helen, is she yours? Or does she belong to one of you other girls?" Ma's brogue thickened, agitation rising.

The basement door creaked, and Donald Sullivan appeared, wiping down a weathered leather satchel. He paused in the doorway, eyes sweeping the room until they met Ma's.

"Donald! Where in the hell have you been? Have you met this woman?" Ma demanded.

Crow's brow furrowed. "What woman, by thunder, are you yammerin' about?"

"The one standin' right in front of you, General," Ma snapped. "Well? Who does she belong to?"

Donald squared his shoulders and turned to Doc. "What's your name, lass?"

Doc lifted her chin. "Fredora Francis Kendall Sullivan."

The room stilled. Ma's eyes widened, then narrowed. "Again, children of mine... who does the *Coill nimfeach* belong to?"

Leonard slipped an arm around Doc's waist. "Ma, the wood nymph belongs to me."

Ma's gaze sharpened. "So, girl, do you belong to the Sullivans of Boston, New York City, San Francisco... or Bellevue, Nebraska?"

Leonard grinned. "None of the above, Ma. She's my wife. We got married a little over a week ago."

Silence crashed down like a falling tree. Ma's eyes grew saucer-sized, and she spun toward Donald. *"Tá bean, gnaoi athair, gnaoi mac!"*

Doc leaned toward Leonard. "What'd she say?"

"'Like father, like son,'" Leonard murmured.

"Yes, woman!" Donald bellowed. "Like father, like son. I thought we swore never to broach that subject again!"

The air cracked like an old Celtic clash of titans. Donald pointed toward the stairs. "Woman of the house. Downstairs. Now."

Without another word, they stomped down the stairs, the door slamming behind them.

Maxine let out a low whistle. "Holy moly. Ma and Pa ain't had a barnburner like that in ages."

Doc blinked. "How long since their last… uh… lover's spat?"

Helen leaned back. "Shirley, how old are you?"

"Eight," Shirley chirped.

Doc chimed in, "Well, that's a damn long time."

Helen clapped her hands. "All right, everybody! You know your spots!"

Doc frowned. "Spots? What's she talking about?"

Curly grinned. "Like the movies. Oldest gets the front row, next in line behind. Family tradition."

"Harold, get a round of beers—Dad's treat," Bob added.

"And some of Dad's Bushmills!" Harold added.

"Me heard that, boyo!" came the hard Irish growl from below.

Harold's eyes went wide. "Roger that, sir!" he called back.

Doc settled into her chair. "Now what?"

Curly leaned close. "Now? We wait. Any second now, the real fireworks start."

A hush fell as everyone took their seats. Shirley, shooed outside, lingered long enough to lob one last shot.

"Wise guy," she snapped at Curly, "take a sock, tie a knot in it, and shove it where the sun don't shine, buddy boy!"

Curly grinned. "Pill, don't let the door hit your ass on the way out."

Doc chuckled. "That kid… adorable."

Downstairs, the faint clink of glass and the scrape of a bottle on wood broke the silence. Everyone leaned in as the first volley sailed up the flue.

"Siad éalaigh!" Ma snapped.

"Are you tellin' me or askin' me if they eloped?" Donald's voice rumbled back. "Mary Magdalene, my darlin', why cry such a thing? You should be happy."

"A dhéanamh tú smaoinigh sé teileagram mé a colúr ag iarraidh mé cead?!" Ma fired back.

"Do you think he sent me a pigeon telegram askin' permission?!" Donald echoed.

Then Ma's words cut through the air like a knife: "Raiteog, bandraoi, le fuil ar uirthi lámh!"

Leonard's face drained of color. "Holy crap. She just called you a tart, a druidess… with blood on your hands."

Doc blinked. "Wait… am I the tart, the druidess, or the bloody hands?"

Leonard grinned. "All three, love. My bloody tart druidess."

"That's not stretching the point!" shot back Doc.

"I've only had one week of tart," said a happy Curly.

"You mean one week of farts," Doc teased.

"Oh hell, I think Pa struck a chord," Jack muttered as all heads turned toward the flue—all except Doc, who threw back her drink.

"Another drink, Darling?" Curly asked, already reaching for the bottle.

"Yes, please! Something stronger this time," Doc said, pushing her empty glass toward him. "In fact, I'll come with you."

Curly grinned and took her hand, leading her to the kitchen. He pulled down a bottle of bourbon from the cabinet, grabbed two glasses, and set them on the counter.

"Pour me a stiff one," Doc said.

"You got it, Doll," Curly replied, handing her the glass and stealing a quick kiss.

Across the room, Rita leaned toward her sisters. "Your brother," she whispered, "'Sé tá a foirfe asal.'"

Helen chuckled. "Remember, she's a horse doctor who married a jackass. He *is* a perfect ass."

"Your mom's blood pressure looked a little high," Doc observed, glancing toward the flue.

Curly nodded. "Marriage catches her off guard. She's all about old-fashioned Irish weddings. Give her time—it's a sore subject for some reason."

"B'fhéidir sise tá le leanbh?" Maxine whispered.

"Maybe she's with child?" Helen echoed, brows lifting.

"Chun shanghai a fear?" whispered Rita.

"To shanghai a man?" Helen murmured back.

"Sise tá a mactíre sa caorach éadach," Maxine added.

Rita nodded thoughtfully. "She *is* a wolf in sheep's clothing. There's something bold about that woman… can't put my finger on it."

"Sise tá ar an teith," Helen muttered.

"You think she's on the run?" Maxine asked, eyes widening.

"Scaoilte beathú, scaoilte moráltacht," Rita murmured.

"Loose living. Loose morality," Helen translated quietly.

"Bhur amadán de a deartháir," Rita muttered, shaking her head.

"Your fool of a brother," Maxine echoed, lips pursed.

Helen sighed. "I just hope he knows what he's getting into."

***

"Chomh, sé cosúil sé gnaoi a chuid athair," Ma's stern voice floated up the flue.

"Take your seats—they're back at it," Rita said, dropping into her chair.

"Mom just said, 'So, it seems he is like his father,'" little brother Dickey translated.

"Sé tá ar bith smaoineamh le haghaidh a chuid máthair," came Ma's sharp tone.

"He has no thought for his mother," Bob muttered.

"Péinteáilte raicleach," Ma snapped.

Helen leaned closer. "Mom just called Leonard's new wife a painted jezebel."

"Hey, sis—we're right here," Curly called.

In hard Gaelic, Ma's voice cut through the flue: *"Míchuíosach béas."*

"Extravagant habits," Leo translated, grinning.

"Na sóisialta dréimire."

"The social ladder," Harold added.

"Sise sá í féin ar é."

"She thrust herself upon him," Curly translated in a WC Fields's imitation.

"Well, hell's bells… my turn," Jack said. "Ma just said, 'She has made my life miserable.'"

"Boy, oh boy," Bob muttered. "'Her wicked little heart,' Ma called her."

Dickey cleared his throat. "And last one: 'He did it behind my back.'"

Through the flue, Pa's voice thundered in old Gaelic: *"Caile cuirim a clár ar sé."* Then silence.

Jack blinked. "Holy moly… Pa just blew a cork. He told Ma to put a lid on it."

"What kind of bad habits do you have on that social ladder?" Maxine teased.

Rita grinned. "Curly, when she thrust herself upon you, did it hurt… or was it an interlude?"

Curly's eyes widened, but Doc answered first. "It was an interlude. Darling, another drink, please."

"Honey, that little ornery nonsense is making your eyes well up," Curly said quietly as they headed back to the kitchen.

"No, not at all, Darling," Doc replied, swirling the bourbon in her glass.

"Then what is it?"

"Just thinking about everything that's happened in the last four weeks."

"Second thoughts?" Curly asked, voice softening.

Doc smiled. "God, no."

"Well, the best week has been with me," Curly said, nudging her shoulder. "So, what gives, buddy boy?"

Doc met his gaze. "I'll tell you later."

From the other room, Helen hollered, "Hey, Curly! Did you really let her guide you?"

"No, Sis—it was half-and-half," Curly called back.

He grinned at Doc. "Bunch of dandies, aren't they? But they grow on you. They'll bend over backward for you because you're family."

"And don't buy that blarney about you making Ma's life miserable," Curly added. "I grew up with her."

A small voice piped up from the doorway. "Hey, Lady Doc… is your heart really wicked?"

Doc smiled down at the child. "No more than yours, kiddo."

Curly leaned in with his best W.C. Fields impression. "By the way, ankle biter, report just came in—your dog's walking your doll down Pennsylvania Avenue. Grab the keys, take the Studebaker. Might need a book under your butt. And double clutch… don't let the door hit your ass."

Laughter rippled through the room as Ma's voice floated up once more from below, sharp as ever. Pa's rumbling reply followed— quieter, but steady.

Curly poured another round. "See? They'll yell, they'll curse… but it's all part of the dance."

"That gave me the heebie-jeebies," said Helen, her eyes wide. Everyone else sat saucer-eyed, except for Curly, who leaned back, waiting for the inevitable.

"This is what Mom just said," Curly explained, grinning. "'Donald, my darling, don't act like a billy goat. Put that in your pipe and smoke it.'"

The room chuckled, but Curly held up a hand. "And Dad fired back, 'My darling warhorse, you want me to smoke your middle finger?'" He shook his head, laughing. "Then Dad added, and I'm quoting here, 'I don't understand French.'"

From the basement flue, Ma snapped, "Gluaiseacht chun na diabhal. Tú tocaim aois práta!"

Maxine snorted. "Go to the devil, you wrinkled old potato."

"Dún bhur gob torchaire, waif. Mo cloigeann goil!," Pa shot back without missing a beat.

Leo translated, "Shut your mouth, wife… my head hurts."

"Mé mian a dhéanamh sé cathain na spiorad bogann mé," Ma retorted. Then silence.

Bob leaned forward. "That was the one-two combo. She told him, 'I'll do it when the spirit moves me.'"

From below, the General's voice boomed: "Woman of the house! The eventualities of war are upon us. There's a great storm brewing. America is on the verge of war, my old love. Leonard and his brothers are in the Army."

Upstairs, necks snapped toward Leonard. Raymond spoke first. "I suppose you can't—or won't—explain what Pa meant?"

"Yeah, Curly. What gives?" Jack added.

"What's the skinny?" Harold pressed.

"Spill the beans," Bob urged.

"What's the lowdown?" Leo asked, brows raised.

Maxine crossed her arms. "Curly, is that why you've been gone so much lately?"

Curly sighed. "Something like that, Sis."

Doc leaned against the counter. "Darling Abercrombie, Raymond's asking if you're planning to divulge what you've been up to."

Leonard grinned. "You mean disseminating highly classified military information? Sure, why not?" He paused, then shrugged. "Sorry, boys. No can do. Loose lips sink ships. You know the drill— ears and eyes only." He glanced at Doc, his smile softening. "I'd be Cain to my five Abels if I let anything slip."

The flue rattled again.

"My love, collect your thoughts," the General's voice rumbled. "Let's say no more—for their sake."

Mary Magdalene's voice followed, quieter but firm. "We'll go to early church, pray for the boys… and all the other soldiers. What am I to say to her?"

The General didn't hesitate. "Start with an apology. After that rash judgment and narrow-mindedness you showed toward that woman… well, you were ranting and raving, Mary."

A pause.

"There's a rude awakening in store for him," Mary Magdalene muttered.

The General chuckled. "And how's that, my little Irish Spring?"

"He'll have to cook his own meals, clean his own boots, and darn his own socks while she's off working at the hospital," she replied, matter-of-fact.

"Let's head upstairs and warn the kids… looks like there's a breakfast wedding ahead," Pa said, his voice softening. "How does she strike you now?"

The General sighed. "A lot harder than your weak blows." He chuckled. "But she's very attractive. Your boy could've done worse. I'm proud of him."

"Donald Leo Crow Sullivan! Ye still owe me a proper Irish weddin'—with the wealth o' me dowry an' all me belongin's that were never bestowed upon me 'cause o' the arrangement with me brother, the great mad Anthony Waugh," declared Mary Magdalene.

"I just heard the door," said Maxine.

Ma emerged from the basement stairwell, smoothing her dress and brushing a hand across her hair. She stood tall, chin lifted. Pa followed a few steps behind, silent as he stuffed tobacco into the bowl of his pipe. Without a word, he lit it, walked to his chair, and sat down carefully. He puffed from his pipe and said, "Remember, my love, I bought you from him. He was going to make you a whore."

Ma's gaze moved from Pa to Doc. "My dear girl, I owe ye a proper apology. I've got a sharp temper when surprises catch me off guard—'specially big ones."

She stepped forward, reaching for Doc's hands. "Here, give me yer hands. Let me look at ye, now that ye're part o' the Sullivan clan. Now that ye're me daughter, ye can just call me Ma, mo leanbh… me new child."

Ma turned Doc's hands over, examining them thoughtfully. "My, for a doctor, yer hands are rough. Like ye've worked the fields—a shovel, maybe? Always somethin' in yer hands other than a scalpel." She glanced up, sincerity softenin' her features. "From the bottom o' me heart, I do apologize, me child. Sometimes, I'm a blunderhead. But yer father-in-law? He's a nitwit. Don't forget that, sweetheart."

Doc smiled. "No harm, no foul. Looks like I got the best of both worlds."

Then, with a mischievous glint, Doc added in old Celt, "Sa fhuil uile a chuid lochtanna, tú fós grá é."

Ma's eyes widened. "So, Doctor… 'In spite o' all his faults, ye still love him.'" Her head tilted curiously. "Where did ye learn the old tongue, me dear?"

"Dr. Katie Quinncannon. We went to medical school together… then took an actual slow boat to China," Doc said, chuckling.

The General, who had been listening quietly, spoke up. "Where in China, exactly?"

Doc folded her arms. "Started in Nanjing—didn't stay long. That was December 1937. We had to take a powder by early '38. About thirteen of us made our way to Kashgar, in western China."

The General's brow furrowed. "Well now… that's quite interestin'. May I see you and yer dapper husband in me study, please?" He gestured toward the hallway.

Curly exchanged a glance with Doc, then nodded. They followed Crow into the study, and Curly quietly shut the door behind them.

Crow leaned against his desk, arms crossed. "Little lady, what's this about Kashgar, China… from 1937 to, let's say, ten days ago?"

Doc blinked. "What about it?"

The General's voice lowered, eyes sharp. "Let me ask ye an important question, Missy. Straight to the point… what did ye see in an' around Kashgar?"

CHAPTER 2 - BREAKFAST

"Well, General Sullivan, I saw quite a bit—more than I bargained for," said Doc, adding, "We played hit-and-run with the Japanese. They're buildin' up a large force of infantry, tanks, airplanes, railroads, ammo dumps, and other installations southeast of Kashgar."

"Hit-and-run?" asked an inquisitive General Sullivan.

"Yes," Doc confirmed. "Ambushes, capturing prisoners, takin' out sentries… those little yellow rays of sunshine."

"Young lady!" the General snapped. "I don't need to hear another word. Have ye told anyone else about this information?"

Doc shrugged. "Why yes, I told me beautician, a bartender, and a fortune teller."

The General's eyes widened like saucers—then he burst into a loud, boisterous laugh. "Could ye be a good little darlin' and go have a chat with yer new mother-in-law for me sake?"

"Pops, what gives?" asked Curly.

"She's a godsend! When ye tuck in for the night, tell her she's goin' to a meetin'."

"With all due respect, sir, is that a request or an order?" asked Curly, standing straighter.

"A little bit o' both, son… but leanin' toward friendly persuasion," the General replied with a wink.

"Alright, everybody, off to bed now—mind ye, no shenanigans. We've got a weddin' breakfast to prepare for. Except you, Doc," said Ma as everyone trailed off, leaving Doc and Ma behind to get acquainted.

"Damn, what time is it?" Doc grumbled, rubbing her eyes.

"Five-thirty," replied an equally sleepy Curly.

Doc sniffed the air. "What smells so damn good this fine mornin'?"

Curly chuckled. "Most likely yer unfavorable wind last night. Omaha stockyards had nothin' on ye—ye sounded like Benny Goodman's clarinet, blowin' licks and riffs, followed by a Gene Krupa drum solo. Sing, Sing, Sing, straight from yer backside." He eyed her playfully. "Quite the concerto—toot, toot, toot."

Doc scowled. "Real funny, wise guy."

Curly grinned wider. "By the way, honey, how many cases did you and Ma polish off last night? 'Cause Bushmills makes yer wind smell fetid... bad enough to turn a man's stomach."

Doc rolled her eyes, combing her hair. "We had a little Bushmills. And yer point bein'?"

"Oh, nothin'. Just thinkin' you'll fit right in," Curly teased, shit-eatin' grin firmly in place.

"That pleasant smell?" Doc asked, sniffing again.

"Thank God, that's Ma's cookin'," Curly said. "Well, Mrs. Sullivan, ready for yer weddin' breakfast?"

Doc stretched. "Ready? I'm as ready as I'll ever be, Mr. Sullivan."

Curly straightened his tie. "Here, love, check me tie, please. And thank ye, ye little vixen." He leaned in, voice dropping. "I need to explain somethin' about the old man. If the Army's his main course, the Nebraska Cornhuskers football team is dessert. I think he loves them more than his own kids."

Doc chuckled. "That tracks."

"He's got this game he's played for years… 'Name the Future Nebraska Football Coach.' If it's a good pick, the old man's already thought of it—or he'll steal it on the spot."

Curly gave Doc's waist a playful squeeze. "How ya feelin', my love?"

Doc yawned. "I could use some hair of the dog, a cigarette, and three aspirins. In no particular order."

"Doc, ye sit at the head of the table. Go on, take me own seat," said Crow. "Mother Sullivan, what's for the weddin' breakfast?"

Ma clapped her hands. "My darlin' Leonard, we're havin' the grandest Catholic-non-Catholic weddin' reception with the finest food an' drink. I asked Pat an' Doris to come over an' help this mornin'."

"Mary Magdalene," said the General, "name off the menu an' have the girls place everything proper."

"We've got fried eggs, scrambled eggs, poached eggs, white an' black pudding, hashbrowns, liver, bacon rashers, pork sausages, sautéed mushrooms, baked beans, fried sliced tomatoes, soda bread, Irish breakfast tea, and some creamy colcannon!" Ma announced as each dish was placed strategically in front of Doc.

"Mind ye, we're not tippin' the table," Rita quipped. "New in-laws get it 'in aice sean-nós agus dlí.'"

"By traditional custom and law," Curly translated.

The General grinned. "Here, new daughter-in-law, have a big gob of colcannon to put in yer gob." He scooped a generous spoonful onto Doc's plate.

"Take yer bacon, pass the plate. Give her some liver. Do ye like scrambled or fried eggs? Let's go, Missy—no BS at chow time!

There's fourteen of us here. Pass those plates after ye've gotten yer share," barked the General.

"That was good," said the General, very satisfied.

CHAPTER 3 - COACHES

"Now, who's come up with new names for future Nebraska Cornhuskers head coaches?" said the General. "Who? That's my first sucker," he added.

"Pops," said little Dickey, "I've been mulling over the name Callahan as a future coach's name."

"My youngest son, that's the Waugh side talking. When you've come to your senses and graduated West Point, all that nonsense will be gone," said the General, adding, "Callahan," while running his index finger across his throat. "Is that all? No other combatants or putzes!?"

"Yes, sir, right here!" said Ray, adding, "Devenny."

"Devenny?" the General bantered. "Young man, you weren't even a gleam in me eye!"

"It's going to be Devaney, with an 'a.' I have a ledger in me study with dates, times, and names in me desk drawer," said the General.

"No problem, sir. I stand corrected!" said Ray.

The General sat back in his seat with a look of satisfaction on his face.

"Do you see what I mean about the old man? You can't win with him!" whispered Curly to Doc.

"Osborne. Osborne, with an 'e.' That was the other one I picked along with Devaney. Or there could be Frost in hell! I don't care.

Any of these Irishmen will try to lead us to a mythical national championship in football," said the General.

"What about Riley?" said Leo.

"No, I don't think so, son," said the General, pinching his nose between his fingers. "And once we get the coaches, the players will follow. Just like this young man out West," he added. "Boys, two years ago, with a few pennies, I bought an illustrated football annual dated from 1936 to 1940. But the 1939 one caught me eye! In 1939, UCLA had a young man out of Pasadena Junior College. The article was written by…" The General stood up and shuffled the papers in a desk drawer. "Here, let me find it. Where's me glasses?" he muttered.

"Here they are, Dad," said Max.

"Thank you, darling. The man's name is Braven Dyer. The young man he was talking about? Jack or Jackie Robinson, born in Cairo, Georgia. Then the Robinson family moved to Pasadena," said the General, reading the article.

"Now, Mr. Dyer, these are his words, not mine," he continued, reading aloud to the family.

"Bruin rooters are strutting happy over the enrollment of Jackie Robinson, one of the greatest ball-carrying prospects in Coast history. Hailing from Pasadena Junior College, the colored fireball will be eligible for immediate varsity competition. Robinson's presence resulted in crowds from 30,000 to 60,000. Competent critics rate him the fastest man in football today," read the General.

"Mr. Wilton Hazzard said, 'Young Mr. Robinson's scissor legs gained a nifty 12 yards from the scrimmage line. He was the top man in punt returns, netting 20 yards per gallop. This fall, he is budding into a triple-threat operator, having added punting and passing to his repertoire. Terrific speed, a 25-foot broad jump, ability, and a baffling change of pace make him, by every appearance, a nightmare for the opposition,'" the General concluded.

The General looked up from the article. "Now those are the kind of men and women that need to come to the University of Nebraska to get the greatest education and security. That's the key to everything in life. It also doesn't hurt to have the greatest sports programs, too. And if not, it's the Marquis of Queensberry rules," said the General with a big grin.

"Capt. Sullivan!" the General called, and six captains turned to face him. "At least West Point taught you six shooters something," he chuckled. "I need the low middle son," he added.

"Honey, what is your father talking about?" asked Doc.

"There are six of us—Leo and Harold, are the high sons, myself and Ray are the middle sons, and then Jack and Bob are the low sons," explained Curly.

"That's quite a family secret," said Doc.

"I need this Capt. Sullivan—my son Leonard—and my lovely new daughter-in-law in my study," said the General. "Close the door behind you, son."

From outside the study, Rita's voice rang out. "Ma, Ray and Jack tried to fart at me!"

"Do I have to cut me a switch? Because when you were little, I made you cut your own! And there'll be no supper tonight!" said Mary Magdalene in her Irish brogue.

"Helen?" called Harold.

"Yes?" she answered.

"Jack and I got some of that special candy for you!" said Harold.

"So, little lady," said the General.

"Well, sir, I guess I'm all in," said Doc.

"Well, me darling, what I say from now on is strictly top secret. Do you understand the gravity of that? Do I make meself clear?" said the General, looking at his daughter-in-law.

Doc nodded, holding his gaze for a moment.

"Then it's settled. No time for a nap. Pack your crap—we're leaving now," said the General.

"Where are you going?" asked Doc.

"You're coming too, darling," said Curly.

"If I told you, I'd have to give you a fatherly kiss on the cheek, like one of me daughters," said the General. "Son, go tell your brothers and sisters goodbye, and leave Mother for last."

Doc and Curly followed the General's orders, saying their goodbyes. Doc slowly approached her mother-in-law.

"Ma, what can I say?" she whispered.

"I understand, daughter-in-law. We had a good long talk, and that will suffice me for now—until you, Leonard, and the grandbabies come home," said Mary Magdalene, wiping tears from her eyes.

"I'm off to church, to give prayer and thanks that you are safe wherever your journey carries you!" said Mary Magdalene. She hugged her son and daughter-in-law. Doc made the rounds to the brothers and sisters, wiping away tears as they walked out the door.

"Here's me driver, Sgt. Bonnie," said the General, introducing Doc and Curly with a gesture toward the car and the man in the front seat.

"Where to, sir?" replied Sgt. Bonnie.

"Mr. Bonnie, hit her in the shitter! Like old Colonel Ritter," said the General. "Normally, we'd go to the Munitions Buildings, but this is much, much bigger than that. Off to the White House, man."

"There's finally rumblings of a brand-new building. They'll build their building, and we will fight the war," said the General.

The car stopped at security, where an armed MP approached and looked inside at the occupants. "Identification, please."

General Sullivan rolled down the back window and handed the officer his identification badge. "I'll vouch for these two. This is my son, Captain Leonard Sullivan, and his wife, Dr. Fredora Sullivan."

"Thank you, General," the MP said, rendering a hand salute and standing at attention. "Please carry on, sir."

The General returned the salute and said, "Proceed, Sgt. Bonnie."

The car cleared security and approached the east wing of the White House. Sgt. Bonnie stopped, got out, and opened the doors for General Sullivan, Captain Sullivan, and Doc, who all stepped out.

"Sgt. Bonnie, go find a place to smoke a cigarette. There's a wee bit of business that needs attending to," said the General.

Sgt. Bonnie drove off as the group turned to meet an aide.

The General addressed the aide. "I'm here for my 1:00 p.m. meeting with the President."

The aide nodded. "Yes, sir. The President is waiting for you." He guided the group along the marble colonnade to the Oval Office.

"Remember, you two—let me do all the talking. They don't know your lovely bride is here," said the General.

"First of all, sit your keisters right here and don't touch anything. I've got a private meeting with the President to discuss some other important issues. I shan't be too long," said the General.

"Darling, you impetuous fool! What did you get us into?" said Doc, scrutinizing her husband's face.

"Honey, it's you they want," said Curly.

"I'm not digging that well! So what gives, sweetheart?" said Doc.

"I'll make a deal with you. I'll tell you now what I was doing in China and what's in the old bag," said Curly, as Doc's eyes grew wide.

"And just to seal the deal, we'll play doctor and patient," Curly added with a huge grin.

"And honey," Curly continued, "from now on, I'll take my temperature the new way—in my mouth, not with the horse thermometer. Thank you."

Doc's eyes widened further, and her mouth hung agape.

CHAPTER 4 - MEETINGS

"General Sullivan, the President will see you," said the President's secretary.

"Thank you," said the General as he proceeded to enter the President's office and took a seat.

"General Sullivan," said the President from behind the Resolute Desk. He seemed larger than life, even seated in his wheelchair.

"How is Mary Magdalene?" asked the President.

"Not bad for the condition we're in!" said the General.

"Sir, have you given any more thought to what we talked about?" asked the General.

"Tell me again what this proposal is," said the President.

"It's combining all the services under the Army," said the General. "As you can see, sir, we have the Army Air Corps—they'll transport the men. We've been looking into utilizing paratroopers for behind-the-lines missions, such as destroying communications and seizing airfields. But the Navy, sir..." The General paused, walked from the corner in front of the desk to the President's side, and leaned in closer.

"Sir, the Navy can hold more men, equipment—tanks, fighter planes, trucks, jeeps, food, blankets, medicine," said the General.

President Roosevelt reached for his cigarette holder, inserted a cigarette, and lit it with a silver lighter. He took a long draw and said, "Go on, General."

"Sir, then there's the Marines. Your very own, bless the little darlings. They can tag along and learn from the Army. Some can scrub the barnacles off the sides of the ships to make them go faster. So if we get into a fracas, we'll get out quicker. That's no blarney, sir," quipped the General.

"So, sir, you can see the need for the Army to be in charge of all the other services," said the General as he sat back in his chair, confident and self-assured.

"Well, General Sullivan," said the President, "it all sounds well and good. But, and there's always a but..." The President paused, took another puff of his cigarette, and continued, "Well, son, Betty Stark, Kelly Turner, and Chester Nimitz already came in together and ambushed me.

"Needless to say, they were quite steamed," said the President.

"Sir, let me ask you," said the General. "How steamed were they?"

"Well, if we were to get on the USS Savannah at 11 a.m. with a full head of steam—which they had—we'd leave the Potomac, head to the Chesapeake Bay, then to the Atlantic, follow the East Coast to Colon, Panama, take the canal to the west side, come out at Balboa, up the west side of Central America past Mexico to Puget Sound of Washington, stop at Senator Wellgren's residence for a 15-minute talk on a new bill he proposed, pick up some very nice flowers for the Mrs., come back the same way, and still get back to the White House with 10 minutes to spare before lunch," said the President.

"And when I got back from the trip, there were telegrams from Bull Halsey and Ray Spruance expressing their displeasure," added the President.

"I—I had no idea," said General Sullivan, his expression shifting from joy to dejection. "That they would take it so personally."

"General Sullivan, is there some other matter you want to discuss with me?" asked the President.

"Very urgent," said Sullivan. "Sir, may we speak frankly? I heard that General Holcomb said Americans of African descent have no right to serve in the Marines."

"If the Marine Corps were 5,000 men who were white or 250,000 who were Black, Holcomb would go with the whites," said the General.

"Sir, we're in the midst of a world war—much larger and deadlier than the Great War. We're going to need everybody. I mean every able-bodied man. We can't afford segregation like the first war," said Sullivan.

Roosevelt snuffed out his cigarette, put the butt in the ashtray, and lit another, taking a long draw. He looked at the General and shook his head slowly.

"My whole life, I've lived off actions, deeds, and words. In and out of uniform, those actions, deeds, and words determine a person's worth," said Sullivan.

"So, General Sullivan, what would you like me to do?" asked the President.

"Sir, you are the Commander-in-Chief," said Sullivan. "I could go old-fashioned, send my second, General Shea, with a silver salver, and we can pull blouses with General Holcomb," he added with a shit-eating grin.

"No, no need for that. As a matter of fact, I'm drafting a measure—Executive Order 8802—that will prohibit discrimination in the defense industry," said the President.

"Sir, we need men on the lines, as well as men and women in the defense industry," said Sullivan.

"One day, the military will be integrated, and I'll be there to see it," said the General.

"But the main topic of these meetings is what's going on in Western China!" said General Sullivan. "We need to get this meeting going and bring all the players in. And, sir, I think we found a ringer!"

The President pushed the speakerphone button and said, "Missy, could you have Capt. Sullivan and his party come into the office, please? Thank you."

"Right away, sir," said Missy.

In this very secret meeting were Henry Stimson, Secretary of War; Colonel Bill Donovan, of the newly formed OSS; President Roosevelt; Capt. Sullivan; Doc; and General Sullivan.

"Mr. President," said General Sullivan, "I'd like to introduce you to my new daughter-in-law."

"And what is your name, child?" asked the President.

"Fedora Kendall Sullivan, or Dr. Sullivan. But my friends call me Doc."

"Well, Doc it is," said the President.

"General Sullivan," Mr. Stimson interjected, "you know this meeting is highly classified?"

"Mr. Secretary, I fully realize that. That's why I brought her along. She has a wee bit of valuable information that just came to my attention in the last two days," said the General.

"And what information would that be?" asked Colonel Donovan.

"All the strategic information from Karachi, China," said the General.

"So, General, by that, I take it Capt. Sullivan didn't get the information we need?" asked Colonel Donovan.

"Tell me, where does Mrs. Sullivan fit into all of this? I'm slightly confused," said Secretary Stimson.

"That makes two of us," added the President.

"Doc?" said the President, turning to address her directly.

CHAPTER 5 - SHIPS LOG

"Doc, make this easy. Tell us what you know, starting from the beginning," said the President.

"Thank you, sir. May I smoke?" asked Doc.

"Don't let me stop you," said the President.

"I went to Johns Hopkins Medical School, graduating in June of 1937. The first week of November, five of us—Dr. Katie Quinncannon, Dr. Betty Brown, Dr. Sue Wang Lee, Dr. Hilda von Haag, and myself—talked for months about going to China. We decided to go to Nanjing, which is where Dr. Sue Wang Lee is originally from.

"Our intention was to start in Nanjing. We rock-paper-scissored a direction, then worked our way through villages, setting up clinics, examining the old and sick, delivering babies, performing needed surgeries, and dispensing medicine," said Doc.

"We packed our belongings and boarded the New England States train from Boston to Cleveland, then to Chicago, where we picked up the City of Los Angeles train. That took us from Chicago to Omaha, Ogden, and finally Los Angeles," Doc continued.

"The five of us stayed a week in Los Angeles. Dr. Lee sent a telegram ahead, so we waited for the reply from an old acquaintance of hers, Dr. Robert Wilson. Two days later, he replied, saying hostilities between the Chinese and Japanese in Shanghai were getting tumultuous. He suggested we stay put," said Doc.

"We looked at each other and said, 'What the hell! We're going anyway. We'll see if we can help,'" Doc added, exhaling a long stream of smoke.

"We booked passage on a very slow tramp steamer called the *Indigo*, Dutch registry, captained by Stephan Schyuler," said Doc.

"We steamed out of Los Angeles, stopped in Hawaii, then headed to Nanjing, China," she finished, glancing at her husband.

***

"We got more than we bargained for. About a mile before port, two Japanese destroyers—the *Akikaze* and *Tachikaze*—told us to heave to. Then they boarded us on December 12, 1937," said Doc, her eyes narrowing.

"That's when I met Major Mugen Mo, a Marine in the Special Naval Landing Forces, and his little aide, Capt. Ronin Kato," Doc added. "It was the first of three meetings."

She took a deep breath and looked around the room.

"Gentlemen, sit back and listen. It's a long story, so smoke 'em if ya got 'em."

CHAPTER 6 DOC'S STORY...

Katie Quinncannon noted, "Girls, I think we're slowing down. I hear some commotion on the ship," her sweet, sassy voice tinged with an Irish brogue. Her piercing blue eyes grew stark and concerned against her coal-black hair.

Suddenly—BANG! BANG!—on the berth door.

"Ladies, I must report that the Japanese Navy is telling us to heave to," said Capt. Schuyler.

"The Japanese and Chinese have been at war since July. It's now early December, and they want to board her. Reports have surfaced that they'll remove all Chinese workers—of which there are 14—below deck. I see no alternative," said Capt. Schuyler.

"I only have a few minutes before they board," the captain added. "My first mate, Mr. Marcus, will take Dr. Lee and the other women to some well-hidden areas of the ship. She'll be safe for now, until we get to port. Would you all please stay in this berth?" said the captain, as the girls looked dumbfounded.

"What are you going to say about the passenger registry?" asked Doc.

"As you say in America, I'll lie my ass off! I'll make something up—like a clerical error," said Capt. Schuyler.

"This feels like all day," said Dr. Betty Brown, a lifelong best friend of Dr. Fedora Kendall. Betty's beautiful, shoulder-length blonde hair framed soft blue eyes.

"Nein, dummkopf! It's only been 20 minutes," said Dr. Hilda von Haag, from one of Germany's best aristocratic families. Also blonde-haired and blue-eyed, she was a little older, having started her medical career ten years later.

Suddenly—BANG! BANG!—on the berth door.

"I'll get it," said Doc.

As she opened the door, she was met by Major Mugen Mo, a samurai. They stood eye to eye—5'9", 165 pounds. His cropped military haircut against tanned skin made his black eyes look as empty as a cave. Brown boots, pristine green trousers, and a pressed green jacket complemented his light-colored shirt.

For a small man, his waist wrap held a traditional *Senninbari*, along with a samurai katana and its companion *wakizashi*. A holster secured his standard Nambu pistol. Behind him stood his aide, Capt. Ronin Kato, dressed identically. Both men stood at attention, giving them an air of greater height. Doc stared back silently, her concern growing.

Major Mo sternly addressed the ship's captain: "パスポートを見るために。あなたのパスポートがありますか？"

"Ladies," said Capt. Schuyler, "he's asking to see your passports."

One by one, the women handed their passports to Major Mo.

"どの港を出港し、最終目的地は南京ですか？"

Capt. Schuyler translated, "What port did you leave, and is Nanjing your final destination?"

Without warning, Major Mo backhanded Capt. Schuyler, drawing blood from the corner of his mouth. Then Mo barked at the captain: "美しい白い蝶に自分に言い聞かせたい。"

He slowly ran the back of his right hand down Dr. Brown's cheek.

Dr. Brown, looking down, suddenly landed a whopper of a right cross to Major Mo's nose, stunning him and forcing him a few steps back.

"Back off, Buster! I've had better," she said with conviction.

Major Mo chuckled as he wiped blood from his nose. Then, in a menacing, sadistic tone, he muttered: "私たちはいつか道を渡る。私はパスを再びクロスを確認します。"

Turning to Dr. Brown, he added, "不幸な事故の日に何が起こったのかわかりません。アメリカの船、USSパナイの事件の犠牲者は残念ですが、船が適切にマークされていなかったという話を聞いています。"

The Major turned and walked away, signaling Capt. Kato to follow with Capt. Schuyler in tow.

Katie Quinncannon quickly closed and locked the door.

"Betty," asked Doc, "are you all right, honey?"

"Why yes, I am, but I think I broke a nail. Damn, I'd worked on that one so long," said Dr. Brown, as the girls chuckled.

Dr. Quinncannon rubbed the back of her neck. "Mé fuair a snámhach-driuch mothú," she muttered, then added in English, "I got a creepy-crawly feeling on the back of me neck."

"That was a good sock to the nose," said Quinncannon.

"If he'd touched me, I'd have reported him to Uncle Oskar Trautmann, Germany's ambassador and a close friend of my father's. Our two governments have the Anti-Comintern Pact," added Dr. von Haag, her tone aristocratic and arrogant. "It's an anti-Communist pact, you know."

Doc nodded. "Betty, he mentally raped you. And Katie, you're right—that was very creepy-crawly and sadistic."

Doc lit a cigarette, pulled out her compact, checked her reflection, and adjusted her bangs.

Two large raps on the door startled the women.

Katie opened the door. "It's Dr. Lee and Capt. Schuyler!"

Dr. Lee entered and sat on the edge of the bed. Capt. Schuyler stood in the doorway and reported, "The Japanese are gone now."

"They didn't take any of my crew after I bribed Major Mo. But the four women passengers and their daughters—they were hidden under some boards between the hull and the floor. The Major ordered his men to summarily behead all the husbands and shoot or bayonet their sons in the galley," said Capt. Schuyler.

The women gasped.

"Sue, are you okay?" asked Betty.

"As you Americans say, no worse for wear. But my heart is racing a hundred miles an hour," said Dr. Lee, her petite frame rigid, pretty black hair framing thoughtful black eyes.

"Capt. Schuyler," asked Doc, "what did Major Pain-in-the-Ass say before he dragged you away?"

Schuyler thought for a moment. "I believe he said, 'I want the beautiful white butterfly to tell me herself.'"

The captain paused and added, "He also said, 'I am sure our paths will cross again, my delicate white butterfly.'"

Doc's face hardened. "He mentioned something about the USS *Panay*, didn't he?"

"Yes," replied the captain. "The Major said, 'By the way, an unfortunate accident happened today. The American ship USS *Panay* was sunk. I have no idea about casualties. I heard the ship was not marked properly.'"

"Soon we'll be pulling into port. It's getting dark, which works to our advantage," said Capt. Schuyler.

"I'm sure more Japanese officials will be waiting at the end of the gangplank," said Doc.

The second mate appeared in the doorway, excitement in his voice. "Skipper?"

"Yes, Mr. Marcus?" said Capt. Schuyler.

"The crew is cleaning up the galley, sir," reported Mr. Marcus.

Captain Schuyler looked around, then back at his second mate. "Mr. Marcus, if I remember right, the manifest for Asiatic Petroleum Company lists oil pipes. Crates are marked 'Pipes.' We're going to hide the ladies in the pipes in the hold. There's another shipment marked 'Spare parts for the Nanjing office'—five large crates labeled 'Pipes' in the number two hold destined for the Shanghai office. We'll take all seven crates to Nanjing," said Capt. Schuyler.

"Ladies, you'll be going to Nanjing in a slightly different way. We'll stow all your luggage into the two small containers and put you in the five crates marked 'Pipes.' It'll be a little tight, but you'll be fine after we add more packing material. There are small holes, so you won't suffocate. But remember—stay absolutely silent, especially if we get stopped by the Japanese," said the captain.

"Mr. Marcus."

"Yes, Skipper?"

"Get my brother Jan. Retrieve the second set of ship's logs and manifests. Have Jan make the changes and forge my name. Tell Hans, the radioman, to shortwave old Mr. Cha Ching—they call him the Cash Register," said Capt. Schuyler.

"Tell that old miser we'll pay him double, since he owns the piers. Also, tell him to contact Rev. Black and let him know all the cargo will go to the safety zone," the captain added.

"What safety zone?" asked Dr. Quinncannon.

"As of December 1 this year, the city of Nanjing established a safety zone. The news says an international committee from Germany, America, Great Britain, and Denmark helped set it up. I imagine Rev. Black is there too," said Capt. Schuyler.

"Ladies, remove all your luggage—we're going below decks. The next time you see daylight, you'll be in the safety zone. You'd better visit the powder room now, because it's a long drive to Nanjing," he warned.

Each of the ladies gave Capt. Schuyler a hug goodbye.

At the port, a tall, lanky port authority officer approached Mr. Marcus. "Let me see your paperwork."

Mr. Marcus quietly produced the documents and watched as the officer perused the manifest. The officer handed the papers back. "Your paperwork is in order. You may begin unloading," he said.

Turning to a nearby dock worker, the officer instructed, "Assist these passengers with the transshipment of their cargo."

A container crane lifted each vehicle from the hull and placed it on the dock. The drivers disembarked and joined their vehicles, the precious cargo still hidden away in the trunks.

From the port, the convoy drove into the Nanjing safety zone and parked in a line inside the Nanjing ghetto. The drivers opened their respective trunks. The ladies, entombed for over six hours, stumbled out stiffly. The drivers helped them out, and the women straightened their clothes, trying to tame their hair after the long trip.

"And who are you Fräuleins?" asked Mr. Rabe in a thick German accent.

"Hey, mister, where can a gal visit the powder room?" asked Betty.

"Verzeihen Sie?" asked Mr. Rabe, brows furrowed in confusion.

CHAPTER 7 - SEMPER FI

Fourth Marine Regiment, Shanghai, China, 1937

"Gunny Skidmore," called out Capt. Beans as the gunnery sergeant hobbled into the office.

"Sir, this communiqué just came in from Nanjing," said Gunny, handing the paper to Capt. Beans.

The captain studied it and commented, "Let me guess, Gunny. Our famous Marine mascot Smedley just bit my nuts and shit in my campaign hat?"

"How's that, sir?" asked an inquisitive Gunny, watching as the captain's eyes narrowed while reading the document.

"This communication is asking for four Marines—one officer and three NCOs—to go up to Nanjing and meet a Mr. Rabe, head of the Nanjing Safety Zone. He's vague about the request, only saying there are five packages that need to be removed. I have no idea what he's talking about," said Capt. Beans, rubbing his chin.

Gunny Skidmore thought for a moment. "Let's make this easy. Where's Lt. Boone?" asked the captain.

Just then, a tall figure appeared in the doorway and saluted. "Capt. Beans," said Bromhead Boone.

"I think he's finishing up mess, sir?" interjected Gunny Skidmore.

"Wait a minute, Gunny—he just walked through the door," said Capt. Beans, eyeing Boone. The lieutenant stood 6'3", blonde hair, blue eyes—a St. Paul, Minnesota boy through and through.

"Skidmore, resume your duties," the captain ordered.

"Were your ears burning way up there, Boone?" asked Capt. Beans with a grin as he stood to return the salute.

"Why no, sir. Should they be?" asked Boone, extending his hand. Capt. Beans shook it and handed over the communiqué.

Boone skimmed the paper. "I don't understand this, sir."

"That makes two of us," muttered the captain. "How long have you been here, Lieutenant?"

"Less than three weeks, Skipper," said Boone.

"I'm new here too, Lieutenant," said Capt. Beans, smiling wryly.

"Roger that, Skipper. I'll be right there, sir!" said Skidmore.

"Skidmore, come back in here. How long have you been in a line company?" asked the captain as Skidmore walked back into the room.

"Twenty-four years in Charlie Company, then six years here in Headquarters Company. Got shot by bandits in the knee, sir. They asked if I wanted to go home or take this assignment, and I figured I'd rather keep doing this for the Marine Corps," said Skidmore.

"In your opinion, Gunny, who's the smartest NCO?" asked Capt. Beans.

"That'd be Sgt. Evans," replied Skidmore.

"The strongest?" asked the captain.

"Sgt. Henry. Only thing is, sir, he's all brawn," said Skidmore.

"Sgt. Welch is an outstanding NCO, but he's on mess duty. Sgt. Efird's in the hospital with a broken leg," added Skidmore.

"Alright, let me ask you this—if you were in the worst firefight of your life, who in this regiment would you pick?" asked Capt. Beans.

"Holy shit, Skipper! You should've asked that first. That'd be Gunnery Sgt. Winthorpe Windridge," said Skidmore. "He may only be 5'9", but he's built like an ox. Blue-green eyes, West Texas twang, mean as a rattler."

"With all due respect, sir, that man lives, eats, and breathes the Marine Corps. But don't ever use his first name—those are fighting words!" added Skidmore with a grin.

"And where's Sgt. Windridge now?" asked Capt. Beans.

"The brig, sir. Not in it—he's getting his two favorite leathernecks out of it," said Skidmore as the three men headed toward the brig.

Brig, Fourth Marine Regiment

Gunnery Sgt. Windridge stood outside the cell, arms crossed, eyeing the two men inside.

"Well, here they are—Mo, Larry, and where's my two Curlys? You two outstanding ass-and-holes. It's always one or the other with you—either doing something so stupid you'd fit in the Navy, or half-ass heroic like real leathernecks," growled Windridge, berating Sgt. Chris Reynolds and Sgt. Tom Hook. Both men stood over six feet tall—Reynolds, brown-haired, from Pittsburgh; Hook, blonde-haired and blue-eyed, known as "Hooky" by the company. They were Windridge's prized sergeants—his best in the squad, the platoon, the company, the whole regiment, and maybe, hell, even the entire USMC

"Gunny Windridge," said Hooky, gripping the bars.

"Look at Reynolds, Gunny. He looks like a whole asshole. I'm just a half-asshole," said Hook, still half-drunk, stroking his prized mustache with a shit-eating grin.

"You two pieces of elephant shit. Sit there and shut the fuck up! Nit and your brother Wit," growled Gunny.

"Gunny, did you eat at the mess hall at 4:30 a.m. like usual?" Reynolds piped up.

"What'd you just bark, dog?" snarled Windridge.

"No, I didn't!" snapped the Gunny.

"Well, you should've. Three cups of lifer juice and six Chesterfields by 4:45 might make you feel like a new Gunnery Sergeant," Reynolds teased as Windridge pulled out a pack of Chesterfields.

"Sgt. Reynolds—very soon to be Private Reynolds—got a match?" asked Gunny, holding out his hand.

Reynolds reached into his pocket, pulled out a matchbox, and handed it through the bars.

"Sgt. Hook, come here," ordered Windridge.

Hook stepped up to the bars, and without warning, Windridge struck him across the jaw with the match.

"Fuck! That hurt, Gunny!" Hook barked, rubbing his jaw.

"Does this mean we have to give our stripes back?" asked Reynolds as Gunny blew a long stream of smoke in his face.

"Thank you for sharing that coffin nail with me, Gunnery Sergeant," said Reynolds, unfazed.

Windridge sneered. "Private Hook, if I can strike your face with a match, it means you need a fucking shave, boot."

"You two smell like Chinese vodka—that baijiu bullshit," Gunny continued. "Mr. Big Mouth and his Bigger Mouth Brother. I know it wasn't merriment at Madam Wang's, since most girls say you're limp dicks."

"Which ones, Gunny?" asked Reynolds with a grin.

"Yeah, which one said I'm a limp dick?" Hook teased, grinning as Reynolds shot him a "fuck you" look.

"At ease, maggot shit!" barked Windridge. "How much damage did you two jackasses rack up at Madam Wang's?"

Hook smirked. "One month's pay? Two months?"

"By my count, last year you two worked for Uncle Sam for four months free," Gunny snapped. "You're like the Marine bulldog mascot Smedley—always playing grab-ass, chasing chow and water, and ending up right back in your doghouse—the brig."

Reynolds grinned. "Gunny, I didn't know you could count."

Without missing a beat, Windridge shot back, "At 0400 sharp, myself, you two gutter rats, and the man in the moon with Maggie's drawers on will roll out of the bunk with your junk to dig new latrines for the regiment—and maybe the whole damn Marine Corps."

Windridge grinned widely and rubbed his hands together. "I'm gonna enjoy every minute of this. No passes. A 100-pound potato sack's got your names on it."

He flicked his cigarette butt at Reynolds, hitting him square in the forehead, sparks flying.

Reynolds stared back, not flinching, the burnt ash still clinging to his forehead. "Thanks for sharing the butt, Gunnery Sergeant."

"Why don't you two pretty boys resign from the Corps, shave your heads, stick 'em up each other's asses, and duckwalk backward into the Navy?" growled Gunny. "Be a goddamn burden to some squid eunuch chief petty officer."

"One day, they're gonna make a uniform with ranks you can rip off and on like Velcro," Gunny added with a scowl.

Capt. Beans and Lt. Boone walked into the brig, heading straight for Gunny.

"Sgt. at Arms," barked Windridge.

"Yes, Gunny?" the sergeant replied.

"Let Privates Laurel and Hardy out of their home away from home," ordered Windridge, glaring at Reynolds and Hook.

"Attention!" snapped Gunny, saluting Capt. Beans and Lt. Boone.

"At ease," said the captain. "How can I help you, Gunny?"

"We've got this communication from Mr. Rabe in the Nanjing Safety Zone," said Capt. Beans. "He needs one officer—that'll be Lt. Boone—and three NCOs. That'd be you, Gunny. Who else?"

"Sir, you don't want these two anchor-licking slugs!" Windridge growled. "I was just about to rip their stripes off and shove 'em up their asses. We'll have two new privates by morning, sir. Then I can play rickshaw with my boots stuck in both their asses."

"Gunnery Sergeant," warned Capt. Beans.

"I don't have time for this bullshit," the captain continued. "Gather your gear. Get up to Nanjing ASAP, Lt. Boone. Skidmore will write a pass so I can sign it—that'll get you through the Japanese lines since we're not at war with them. Yet."

"You'll be going by truck," added Beans. "I want American flags on both sides of the trucks. I don't want those trigger-happy bastards mistaking you like they did on the *Panay*. They'll see you're Americans. I hope."

"Lieutenant," said Capt. Beans, "I'm filing this as a three-day field training exercise. Make your way back to cantonment after. Good luck."

"Roger that, Skipper," said Boone, snapping a crisp salute.

Turning to the men, Boone introduced himself. "Lieutenant Bromhead Boone."

***

"So, sir, what's the mission?" asked Reynolds.

"In a nutshell, we're going to Nanjing to transport and protect five packages. Civvies for now, but pack your uniforms," said Boone.

"You two knuckleheads just got amnesty," added Gunny. "Grab all your gear—1911s with full ammo loads, four Chicago Typewriters with 500 extra rounds, four trench 97 shotguns with full loads and extra belts."

Gunny walked off, adding, "Oh, and a full box of 24 grenades. And grab the Bitch—with a thousand rounds."

"What crawled up his ass and died?" muttered Reynolds.

"You did," Hook shot back.

"Yeah, but you helped push," Reynolds replied, grinning.

"By the way, which one of us is Laurel and which one's Hardy?" asked Hook, rubbing his sore jaw.

"Goddamn, my left jaw still hurts," muttered Hook.

"Are we going hunting or range firing with all this ammo?" asked Reynolds.

"Wherever we're going, I hope there's female persuasion. I'm handsome," Reynolds quipped.

"Yeah, you're handsome," Hook laughed. "You're great in a fight, I'll give you that. But it's when you open your fucking mouth, Christopher!"

CHAPTER 8 - AS USUAL

"Did you get all the gear?" Windridge asked Reynolds and Hook.

"Roger that, Gunny," both men reported.

"Get your sorry asses in the back of this truck," snarled Windridge. "This will be a long bumpy ride. I prefer you two double-time behind this truck. Or better yet, I just had an epiphany. You two peckerwoods push the God damn truck at a steady 40 mile-an-hour," slathered the Gunnery. Lt. Boone, looked on with amusement.

"I'm doing nothing for the next 18 hours but ride your dumb asses!" said Windridge.

"Skipper, we buried our weapons, ammo, and uniforms in the back of the vehicle. Roger that, Gunnery Sergeant," said Boone.

Three trucks pulled into the cantonment area. Fifty marines exited the vehicles and lined up in formation as the platoon sergeant inspected their weapons.

"It looks like Capt. Beans cut loose Second Platoon. Almost all the single guys to escort us up to Nanjing. There's Jenkins and Bobby Smith from A Company," said Reynolds .

"Capt. Beans doesn't know how long the Chinese can keep the Japanese out. It's not going to be particularly good for the Chinese," said Lt. Boone.

"Lt. Boone, new orders from the skipper," said Skidmore, handing the new orders to Boone who relayed the message: "Do not return here. Stay with that signed mission until you reach safety, Semper Fi. signed Capt. Beans."

"So, what the fuck does that mean," said Reynolds.

"I wish I could tell you, more Sgt. Reynolds?" said Lt. Boone.

"What of Lt. Smith, of A. Co?" said Hook.

"He has his own separate orders," said Lt. Boone.

"Sgt's. Rumpelstiltskin, and Rumpleforeskin," said Gunny in a calm, peaceful voice.

"Please, gentlemen, put your fists down each other's throat, then say the God damn Chinese alphabet backwards," Reynolds and Hooky listened on with incredulity.

"Sgts. Reynolds and Hook, come over here a minute," said Windridge.

"The Chinese are between a rock and a hard place," Windridge says.

"Here's an early Christmas present for the both of you from Santa and Mrs. Clause and every bellhop and soda jerk in Pennsylvania." Windridge landed a straight shot right in the middle of Reynold's sternum and Hook's jaw. Windridge's force of wrath was on point for both men, as they fell to their knees. "That teaspoon, my friends, came right out of a 55-gallon drum of whoop-ass with your names on it," said Windridge.

Then Sgt. Reynolds pipes up, sucks air in, and says, "*Wunderbar einfach nur verdammt wunderbar,*"

Hook replied, "Yes it was—w*onderful. Just fucking wonderful.*" The two men helped each other up.

"Which Rumple was I?" said Reynolds.

"I am Stiltskin, and your Foreskin!" said a proud Hook.

"Yes, but you have an old wrinkly foreskin. I know old buddy, I have seen it in battle with old Jujube."

"At this moment, my old wrinkly foreskin is in the resting position!" said Hook snickering at his buddy.

***

"Now that we're in the back of this truck, let's try to get some shut eye. It's a long trip Gretel and your ugly sister, Hansel," joked Gunny. "It hasn't even been 15 minutes and one of you sor_s a bitches just shit his God damn civilian uniform, as if you just left Annapolis mess hall and shit all over your whites, Lt., with all due respect, Sir," Windridge said, annoyed.

"None taken, Gunnery Sergeant," said Boone, continuing. "I cannot tell a lie, it was I. I hope you all enjoyed it, because I did," said Boone

Boone smiled widely, relieved. "Sgt. Reynolds," said Boone in a whisper as Reynolds was trying to adjust his ass on the truck floor. "Does Gunny always ride you and Hooky that hard?" asked Boone.

"Only when he wants to do a Dueling Diego on us," said Hook.

"Come again Sgt.?" said Lt. Boone.

"Sir, you'll have to excuse my fellow noncommissioned officer, Sir. When one is as inbred as Sgt. Hook, his brain goes inert," Reynolds laughed.

"Sir, to answer your question, Gunny likes to fuck us at the same time right in Maggie's drawers with the undying passion of fucking us with the Eagle, Globe, and Anchor. It's the fine art of Marine Corps mastery that only Gunnery Sergeant Winthrop Windridge can do," said Reynolds, his voice raised over the noise and commotion along the road.

"Poor Winthorpe." Reynolds slowly rubbed his hand over his face as he and Hook snickered.

"Say LT, Sgt. Hook and I, the two of us had an incident at Madame Wang's House of Pleasure, about five years ago" said Sgt. Reynolds. "A couple of Mdm. Wang's best number one dishes came over with a couple of warm beers. Then they go below deck, Sir, as they say in the Navy. Whoever rolls their eyes first while drinking their beer must pay for the Dueling Diego upstairs," said Reynolds. "Well, Hook one-night yells I won the Dueling Diego's," said Reynolds.

"Jujube was between Chris and I. The three of us were right side up. Then sometimes upside-down, Sir," said Hook.

"That's admirable," said Lt. Boone.

"Yes, Sir. We were in a major campaign doing battle with just our campaign hats on!" said a happy Hooky.

"That's quite an astonishing and interesting tale. You should try it side-by-side in a bed," said Lt. Boone.

"That's what we thought too, Sir," said Reynolds. "Sir, I'm going to tell you a secret story," as he looked toward Gunny's way. "Three weeks ago, Hook and I both had guard duty which is nothing new," said Reynolds, holding his hand up like a megaphone to direct his voice to Boone above the loudness surrounding them.

"As usual," grumbled Hook.

"Sir, before I was rudely interrupted by Sgt. No nuts, we happened to be walking past Gunny's building his smoking lamp was on, the window was partly open, when Sgt. Peeping Tom Hook looked in the window," said Reynolds.

"Fuck you boot, you looked, too," said Hook.

"What we saw there was Gunny at the Head, at position of attention his back was turned to us, he was in his best birthday suit, except his campaign hat on his head with cartridge belt and 45, Sir, and his boots. He was doing a proper Marine Corps salute with his right hand," said Reynolds.

"But his left hand, let me say this Sir, his thumb was not running down the seam of his trousers sir. It's more along the ines. of raising old glory on his flagpole," said Sgt. Hook.

"We both started running, Hook was laughing like a little girl. But then we heard," said Reynolds, mimicking Windridge, "You sorry sons a bitches. God might own your soul, the Marine Corps may own your body, but your blood stripes and balls, you fucking Army rejects, belong to ME. I'm going to take great pleasure killing you both slowly."

"Needless to say, Sir… My nutsack shriveled like a dried persimmon Sgt. Windridge as a lot of kills," said Reynolds. "Since Sgt. Hook is a eunuch, no dried shriveled persimmons for him! And he's lucky Sir, in China they'd take off his little toothpick dick, too!"

"You're so fucked!" Hook said, contorting his face.

The truck ambled along the bumpy road, beeping their horn to clear the masses of refugees. The din of constant screaming in the distance permeated the air all along the route. Bombs were exploding all around them, and flashes of light and fire lit the sky.

"So, Sir, we were thinking wherever this mission is taking us, could you, with all due respect, Sir, run interference, Sir. I know you're new and all, Sir, but it would be well appreciated," said Hook.

Reynolds looked back at Hook and shook his head yes, too.

"So, what you two leathernecks are telling me, you don't want Gunnery Sgt. John Philip Sousaphone inserted up your ass," said Lt. Boone.

"Something like that, Sir," said Reynolds.

"I'll see what I can do," said Lt. Boone.

The men sat silently, listening to the sounds of war and destruction around them as they made their way through Nanjing.

CHAPTER 9 - NANJING

"What time is it?" asked Doc.

"It has to be 5 o'clock somewhere in D.C.," said General Sullivan.

"I could use a stiff belt myself, " said Colonel Donovan.

"That sounds like a wonderful idea," said the President.

"Henry," said the President.

"Yes, Mr. President?"

"Right behind you, Secretary Stimson, in that cabinet open it up and reach back there. You'll find a nice bottle of Bush Mills given to me by General Sullivan on my first run at office," said the President. The bottle was passed around and cigarettes were lit.

***

"Lt. Boone, we're here sir," said Windridge, as the trucks came to a stop inside the Nanjing safety zone.

"I gotta take a two-hump-camel-size piss," said Reynolds.

"That makes two of us," said Hook.

"Sgt. Peeping Tom, you squat to piss, Hook USMC," said Reynolds.

"Fuck you kindly!" said Hook.

"Who is Lt. Boone?" a heavy German accent came from behind the truck.

"That would be me sir," replied Lt. Boone. "And you are?"

"I'm John Rabe, Head of the Nanjing safety zone. We received a communiqué that you were arriving sometime yesterday, today, or tomorrow."

"Sir, what is the name of this place," inquired Boone.

"This is Ginling College campus, presided by Miss Minnie Vautrin," said Mr. Rabe.

"I have to apologize about the time, Sir, the roads are flooded with refugees. We would've been here last night but we couldn't get through, so we found a place to bed down," said Lt. Boone.

"Lt. we must all get inside," said Mr. Rabe.

"Yes, Sir," replied Boone.

"You're lucky to be alive. I need to talk to you in private, Lt. Boone?" said Mr. Rabe. "I'll have my men secure your equipment."

"Mr. Rabe, I need to find Lt. Smith. I'll be right back sir," said Boone.

Boone found Lt. Smith pulling into the college parking lot. Smith got out of his truck and brushed himself off, rearranged his hat, and looked around. Lt. Boone approached him and shook his hand.

"Lt. Smith, I suggest you should stay here tonight and get a fresh start in the morning," said Boone.

"No, we are going to turn around, my orders say we're heading back," said Lt. Smith.

"You should really think about this one," said Lt. Boone.

"That asshole liaison Jap Colonel. I'd like to shove his face in a pile of Smedley shit. His aide was just a bundle of joy too," said Lt. Smith. "Remember I have the flags on the side and top of our trucks. I have my pass to get out of school," laughed Lt. Smith. Boone and Smith saluted and shook hands.

***

"I've slept in better beds," said Dr. von Haag in her very aristocratic way. She combed her long, blond hair, patted a light pink rouge onto her cheeks, and carefully lined her lips in bright red, smacking them on a tissue.

"Hilda, you're never happy with what you have," said Dr. Katie.

"But what about the men in the bed," asked Quinncannon.

"Wouldn't you, like to know, dahling," said Dr. von Haag. "I'll be happy when I find an unknowing old Duke or Archduke. He will instantly fall in love with me!"

Ladies, they've made breakfast for us and I'm famished," said Doc.

"I'll, be there faster than I can fix a boxer's busted nose," said Quinncannon.

"Betty, and Sue. Those two girls must be sleeping in. Betty has always been a sleepyhead," said Doc.

Quinncannon and Doc walked into the cafeteria area of Ginling College, where the tables stood full of morning breakfast items such as Congee rice porridge, crullers, doughnuts, and fresh soymilk. The two women heard young girls' voices laughing and talking, and scurrying toward them from down the hall.

Boone and Windridge tried to find a place to sit along the long tables in the cafeteria. Reynolds and Hook made their way into the corner to observe the cafeteria activity.

Reynolds whispers, pointing at Doc and Quinncannon, "I'll take her and her."

"Which her? You said her and her – that's two," whispered Hook.

"The one with the best Eagle, biggest Globes, then I'll drop anchor," said Reynolds.

"Not too fond of yourself are you, playboy to bilge boy?" said Hook.

Dr. von Haag came into the cafeteria and approached Reynolds and Hook, smiling.

The two boots were about to be seated when Dr. von Haag said, "You two darling Homo sapiens please sit by me," Von Haag said, seductively like Marlene Dietrich. All eyes turned her way.

"So gentlemen, what do you do?" von Haag asked as Reynolds reached ahead and lit her cigarette beating Hook by just a second with his silver lighter.

"Better luck next time, Dahling," said Dr. von Haag, winking at Reynolds.

"We work for an oil company!" said Hook. Every head turned toward him.

"Where in the USA do you come from, Dahling," Dr. von Haag asked, as she allowed a lacy waft of smoke to escape her lips and drift toward the ceiling.

"Pittsburgh, Pennsylvania," said Reynolds, mesmerized.

"The same here," added Hook.

"Yes, it's kind of funny," said Reynolds. "Just a little under two miles apart, but never ran into each other. Grandmothers raised us."

"German grandmothers," said Hook.

"And where are you from?" Reynolds asked, looking von Haag up and down slowly and grinning.

"Outside Hamburg. There, I went three years to Greifswald University Hospital, and then finished my last year of Med School at Johns Hopkins. At the very last minute, I impetuously thought I would go to China, too, which is why we're standing here," said Dr. von Haag.

Dr. von Haag stood and grabbed her handbag. "I'll say this in German, *Lieblinge*. I must go to the ladies' powder room! You'll excuse me please," Dr. von Haag turned and walked toward the lounge, four eyes trailed along as she walked. She stopped and looked back, tilting her head slightly and grinning wicely as she disappeared behind the door.

"See Hooky, she called me *Dahling*, yeah! But, like a master to its dog!" said Hook with a shit-eating grin on his face.

Dr. Katie walked into the room. Her pressed black slacks and flowered blouse and her long black hair glistened as she walked past the windows. All eyes tracked her as she strutted to her destination and sat down gracefully. She tucked her purse next to her in the chair, clasped her hands and leaned forward on the table so she could hear the conversation.

Lt. Boone, Gunny, Doc, and Dr. Quinncannon smiled at her as they sat in silence for a moment.

Across the room, Hook quietly tugged on Reynolds's shirt, and whispered loudly, "Look at Gunny with a twinkle in his eye. He looks like he just got his first 1903 Springfield, and there's Maggie's drawers, Dr. Katie!" whispered Hook, scratching his famous mustache.

"No way he loves the Corps too much," said Reynolds, scratching his not so famous mustache.

Mr. Rabe and Dr. Wilson entered the cafeteria and spotted Lt. Boone, who waved. Mr. Rabe nodded to Boone, and turned to Wilson. "Dr. Wilson, let me introduce you." They made their way to the table and introduced everyone as they stood to shake hands. "Wilson and I would like to have a few words with you all in private," said Mr. Rabe to everyone at the table.

"Dr. Kendall," said Dr. Wilson. "I asked you to stay back in the United States, but trust me, the way things are going, I could use your help. We must get your people out of here. It is not safe here! It is not any day—it is any hour or minute—the Japanese will dissect through Nanjing like a scalpel through warm flesh. We have to get you and the other doctors out."

"Dr. Wilson," said Doc facetiously, "We're to believe Boone, Windridge, Hook, and Reynolds work for the oil company? In what capacity, might I ask? Cleaning up messes?"

In the distance, artillery, bombers, and machine guns pounded the battered city of Nanjing.

CHAPTER 10 - THE EYES MEET

***

"He looks out of his league! He's the St. Louis Browns, and she's the Yankees. His mouth is so wide open he's drawing flies," whispered Reynolds.

"I think he's looking at the chow," said Hook.

Reynolds cut in, whispering, "More like that hot Patootie he's looking at. That by-the-book Marine, as you've seen Gunny, looking at a female. Tsk, tsk. That is against fucking Marine regulations."

Hook whispers, "Let's see where he sits. He's always by himself or with Top or the Sgt. Major in the mess hall. You've got to be fucking me like an eight-hour pass."

"He's… he's being, being gentlemanly?" whispered Reynolds. "Is he pushing her chair in with her in it?"

"Oh, shit, he's sitting, sitting beside her," said Hook.

"Dummy so many names and only 24 hours in a day, and you thought it was the chow, Sgt. Squid?" whispered Reynolds, as he began eating his breakfast.

"So, what did I miss? Anything naughty?" said Dr. von Haag seductively, as Hook won the race to light the cigarette of Dr. von Haag.

Reynolds quickly said, "Dick."

"Is that your name, Dick Hook?" asked Dr. von Haag.

"Yes, ma'am it's Dick Hook," said Reynolds, smiling. Reynolds quietly whispered to Dr. von Haag, "Take a look at our Sgt. and Dr. Katie. What do you make of that," whispered Reynolds.

Dr. von Haag whispered matter-of-factly. "Just by one glance, they need to find a boudoir," said Dr. von Haag. Both Hook and Reynolds ears perked up like a pair of German Shepherds." Dr. von Haag continued, "From a medical standpoint, Dickey, you remind me of the excellent German specimens of our male German race with your blonde hair, the blue eyes. Impressive mustache."

Dr. von Haag leaned over close to Reynolds, "Since Mr. Reynolds here, even brown-haired, brown eyed, but your dirt-brown mustache is not appealing. It reminds me of a Knot Grass caterpillar in England, Darling. But it will suffice," alluded Dr. von Haag. Reynolds gently rubbed his not-so-famous mustache, as his grin turned to a frown, his eyes locked to hers.

"I'm sure you'd like to help a Fraulein; a damsel in distress. I've two large steamer trunks that must be moved," said Dr. von Haag, lowering her eyes and batting her lashes. A smile curved her mouth as both men watched her purse her lips slightly.

Reynolds and Hook looked at each other like they kept their stripes another month. "Ma'am, we can move those steamer trunks, in a Dualing Diego fashion," Reynolds whispered to Hook.

"Well, I'm heading up to my room right now and in a few minutes, you great big strong brutes come up," whispered von Haag, walking away and swaying her hips gracefully back and forth hypnotically.

"The baby blues, the blonde hair and 'stache wins every time, not that corn-in-the-poop brown mustache. Your eyes say you're full of shit, sad, incredibly sad, Squirts," with Reynolds whispering.

"Fuck you, running Smedley breath! We need two bottles of hooch," said Reynolds."

Dr. von Haag, reappeared in front of the men and whispers, "By the way, gentlemen! I've some exceptionally fine German brandy and cognac in one of those steamer trunks."

"*Schütteln Sie ein Bein*," whispered Hook.

"Yes, *let us shake a leg,* Watson, another case to crack," said Reynolds.

"I thought I was Holmes," said Hook.

"No, you're Sgt. Peeping Tom-I-squat-to-piss Dick Watson Hook," said Reynolds.

***

Dr. Kendall rejoined the rest of the party and was escorted by Dr. Wilson and Mr. Rabe. Also accompanying them was a beautiful black-haired female, walking next to Mr. Rabe.

"Mr. Boone, I would like to introduce you to Valentina Brandt," said Mr. Rabe. "Her father was a good friend of mine; he worked for the German government in China for several years. He met Valentina 's mother in Beijing. Poor Valentina 's mother died from complications giving birth."

"She has dual citizenship with Germany and China. Her English impeccable, also speaks and writes Chinese, German, Japanese, her father was fabulously wealthy. He was a shipping, mining, imports, export magnet. But her education was the top priority. Money was no object," said Mr. Rabe.

"For the last six months. She has been with me since her father died. By the way, the situation in Nanjing is growing tense. I want you to take her with you!" said Mr. Rabe catching Boone a little off guard.

"Sir, I have no idea where I'm taking the other five ladies," said Boone.

"I know this is a bit out of the ordinary, but everything is being arranged, plus everything is paid for," said Mr. Rabe.

"Then in the next 24 to 36 hours you will be out of here, so let us talk later on our course of action," reiterated Mr. Rabe.

"I'm sorry for the loss of your father," said Boone, turning to Valentina and taking her hand softly.

"I am, too," said Valentina . "I never knew my mother. I thought Papa would live forever. When I was 15, he sent me off to Germany for ten years of education, the last four at the University of Greifswald for law and business," said Valentina . "I was going to follow in my father's footsteps here in the Far East for the German diplomatic corps, but I have no one now." Valentina's eyes welled and her upper lip quivered, as she composed herself, taking back her hand to smooth her skirt.

CHAPTER 11 - THEY TALK

"I swear! Are you capable of a constructive sentence? The way you have been looking at me—are you having a seizure? You must be missing your six lobes and a grand smidgen of gray matter with your gob so wide open. Boyo, you are drawing horse flies. A trifle of perspiration on your forehead," exclaimed Dr. Katie.

"Why, why, no, ma'am, I'm not," said Windridge. As he was caught off kilter.

"By the way you are looking at me, you've never met anybody from the opposite sex," said Dr. Katie.

"Did, you think I was an *Taispeánadh,"* said Dr. Katie.

Windridge cleared his throat and came back with, "Ma'am, I have no idea what you just said," said Windridge, still lost in vernacular.

"I said I was an *apparition*, a ghost, a spook," said Dr. Katie.

Finally, Windridge took a drink of his coffee, and grumbled in a low voice, "God damn it, this is not, I say again not, Marine lifer juice, or chow par-don me ma'am, speaking of spooks. Have you seen Mo, Larry, and my two Curlys?" said Windridge, with Mark l trench knives in his eyes, and a hard tone in his voice.

"The last time I saw them, they're heading down the hall umbilicaled to Dr. von Haag!" said Dr. Katie. with a grin on her face. Windridge's face went scarlet, then cream as Dr. Katie slid closer to him and whispered into his ear, "If you work in the oil company, I'll kiss the backside of a baby's arse, with that scar from the back of your jawbone, down your neck, and if I looked underneath your shirt. If, I, I, mean you were to take off your shirt in an annual exam, I bet I'd find patched up bullet holes and old knife wounds," whispered Dr. Katie.

Dr. Katie and Windridge's eyes met and they paused.

"Mr. Boone is the boss. You bark at them other two, so if I were to guess, Army or Marines," whispered Dr. Katie.

"Marines," whispered Windridge.

"That's interesting," whispered Dr. Katie. Then she asked in old Celt. "*A dhéanamh siad stopadh bhur gearrann sa na muirí?*" Dr Katie moved in close to Windridge's ear, "In English that means, *Do they check your teeth in the Marines*?"

Windridge looked at her with eyes wide open.

***

"Hook," said Reynolds. "You lost the toss; I'll get on the back side of this steamer trunk!" said Reynolds.

"Semper Fi, do or die," replied Hook.

***

"So, tell me Mr. Boone, do you have any formal schooling," asked Valentina.

"Yes, the Naval Academy, Class of 1930," said Boone. "By the way ma'am, my first name is Bromhead," as they shook hands.

"That is deplorable. Those poor people. I feel so helpless on what is going on outside," said Valentina.

"I know how you feel ma'am," said Boone.

"Do you have family back at home?" asked Valentina.

"Not anymore. My father ran away to parts unknown. My mother died giving birth to my younger sister, who died two days later. I've been on my own ever since," said Boone.

***

"Katie," said Doc from across the long table.

"Dr. Wilson, we're going to look in on the patients here in the safety zone," said Doc, adding, "Have you seen Betty or Sue?"

"No, come to think of it, I have not," said Dr. Quinncannon, adding, "She does like taking her time in the ladies' room. Then there's snail Sue," said Katie as the sounds of more artillery explosions and bombs nearby, punctuated by the screams of people trying to find safety.

"Would you like to join us," asked Doc.

"I would relish that," said Dr. Katie.

Valentina, stands and says, "You'll have to excuse me, I have some paperwork to finish up on my father's behalf," said Valentina .

Windridge stands and moves next to Boone, "Mr. Boone, our two other colleagues, Mr. Laurel and Mr. Hardy seem to be lost. I'm going to find them skipper."

Boone cut in, "Let's, have some more coffee first, Gunny."

"Roger that, Skipper!" replied Windridge. Just as Windridge was about to raise his coffee cup up to his mouth, Reynolds and Hook came in and sat across from Lt. and Windridge. Windridge muttered in a bitter, hard way, "Oh, look it's the carbuncle twins!" He looked at his watch. "Fucking Mo, Larry, and my two Curlys," railed Sgt. Windridge, cutting a hard tone with these words of wisdom. "When we are done with this operation, you two are going right to Master tactical Sgt. old lard-ass Fitzsimmons. You two girls are going to peel potatoes, scrub the barracks floors, mess hall, Top's office, take out every bit of trash. Let us say the next six months, you two maggot-brained idiots, your asses are mine," he said, growing agitated.

Gunnery Sergeant Windridge bent over the table and got face to face with Reynolds, "You're with me, from 6 AM to 10 PM, and you will be digging new latrines for every company in the Regiment."

Gunny turned to Hook, "On top of that, you two pieces of Marine shit, gold bricking, pain in my ass. You will guard the shitters during the night, four hours on, one hour off. Then you will walk the length of your new trench for your time off, do an about-face, and then you and the trench can talk shit, jabber, plan your monthly pay, play mumbly-peg on your free hour," scalded Gunny.

The Dr. von Haag sat down next to Gunny with her purse on her lap. She pulled out her compact powdered her face and fixed her lipstick. She put everything away except her cigarettes and lighter. She put the lighter into Gunny's palm and whispered, "Dahling, could you please light me?" Windridge looked at her exasperated, flipped open the lid and struck the roller to produce a flame, bringing it up to Dr. von Haag's cigarette. She leaned forward to light, and took a deep drag, releasing a long stream of smoke just past Windridge's face.

Hilda returned and sat down carefully at the table. She asked, "What did I miss, and how is my hair, Dahling?"

Windridge rose and grabbed his coffee cup, mumbling to himself, "Not Marine lifer juice."

Hook whispered to Reynolds, "Cadaver boy?" said Hook.

"What the fuck, is a cadaver?" whispered a surprised Reynolds.

"The word from Madame Wang's girls. They know you. They said you're a pencil dick and fucked like a 解剖学教室."

Reynolds looked confused.

Hook coming back, whispering.

"It means *cadaver*," as Reynolds was still a little lost.

"Limp Dick, I did not have the heart to tell you that Gunny was talking *about you with the girls earlier,*" whispered Hook. Then not missing a beat, he said, "What do you do, just lay there?"

"Do you mean to tell me," whispered Reynolds blankly, "That the girls Wing Wang, Lu, Yang, YueChuan, and even old dried up Jujube have come to the conclusion that ME, Myself, and I have been accused of fucking like a dead cadaver?"

"12 honest women of ill repute came to that conclusion in Mme. Wang's house of pleasure that you are guilty in the poor penis production court," whispered Hook as he wiped his famous mustache.

At that moment, the front door and side doors flew open and were filled with Japanese military, with three girls ahead of them.

CHAPTER 12 - MET THE JAPANESE

Entering the front door was one Major Mo with his adjutant Capt. Kato. With Maj. Mo yelling, in Japanese の充電、ここに. Everybody stopped what they were doing and their heads quickly turned toward Major Mo.

Reynolds whispered, "Hey Mo!"

Hook whispered, "Hey Larry!"

Followed by Gunny whispering, "Hey, shut the fuck up, Curlys."

Valentina replied to him," 私は、ベライゾン・ワイヤレス社さんの解釈は、南京の安全ゾーンで充電."

"Mr. Rabe," said Valentina . "I told him that *I'll interpret for you and that you're head of the Nanjing safety zone.*"

Reynolds springs up, and says in German, *"Fräulein Valentina ich möchte mit Ihnen zu sprechen und ich möchte Sie es zu übersetzen sie fangen an was ich sage gehen Sie einfach das Gegenteil."*

Lt. Boone heard Gunny mumble, "Gods of the Marine Corps, I'm going to slowly—oh so slowly—sacrifice him. It will be a sacrifice of 1000 cuts, so many for you, a double ration to me, and some to the Fourth Regiment, the Marine Corps. That will purge the scourge."

Windridge's eyes met Hook's. Windridge whispered, "He dies too, soo very, very slowly," as he slowly rubbed his hands over his face.

Dr. von Haag approached Lt. Boone, and said, "Dahling, Chris said this in German. *Fraulein Valentina I want to talk to them, and I want you to translate it. You'll catch on to what I'm saying. Just give them compliments.* I'll interpret for you," whispered Dr. von Haag.

Lt. Boone answered, "Appreciate that ma'am. I'll let Gunny take care of Herr Reynolds!"

Reynolds turned to Major Mo, and said, "*Fräulein, sagen Sie bitte unseren unterscheiden, militärische Besucher, dass sein Gesicht, sieht aus wie die nachgeburt einer Ziege.*" He looked unconcerned, but shook his head up and down as his right index finger tapped his not-so-famous mustache at Major Mo.

Dr. von Haag, slightly giggling, whispers, "Dahling Mr. Boone, Christopher just told that disgusting man, *his face was goat afterbirth*, and I have to agree with him."

Valentina replied to Major Mo, "彼は、形を保つあなた自身を言う." She turned to Reynolds and replied in German, "*Er sagt, dass sie sich selbst in Form zu halten?*"

Dr. von Haag whispered to Boone, "This is what Valentina, told Chris, "*He says you keep yourself in shape.*"

"Referencing the pigs' afterbirth face," whispered Dr. von Haag.

Reynolds says to Major Mo, "*Er riecht nach, die er in das Arschloch einer Ziege, das heißt, er ist ein, eine Ziege, Riechen ass hole schläf.*"

Reynolds returned to tapping his not-so-famous mustache with his left index finger.

Valentina's eyes got rather large, and she quickly replied back," あなたは 米軍の家族から 軍事には常にされています"

"Mr. Boone, dahling," whispered Dr. von Haag. "This is what dahling Chris said in German to that disgusting pig: *He sleeps in the asshole of a goat, which means he is a goat-smelling asshole.*"

Valentina said to Reynolds, "*Sind Sie von einer militärischen Familie, und Sie haben immer im Militär.*"

Dr. von Haag interpreted, "*Are you from a military family and have you always been in the military?*".

Major Mo replied, " はい 両方の質問に 私の家族は 多くの世代のしているのは *1877* 年（明治 *10* 年）には サムライのようにすることで　城山の戦いをしています。切断されたときにまで もししています。 これらの男性は誰ですか？"

Valentina responded, "*Ja, zu beiden Fragen meine Familie für viele Generationen bis 1877, wenn der Weg des Samurai wurde in der Schlacht von Shiroyama. verloren Und durch die Art und Weise. Wer sind diese Menschen?*"

Dr. von Haag responded, "*Yes, to both questions. My family has been military for many generations, until 1877 when the way of the samurai was lost at the Battle of Shiroyama. And by the way, who are these men?*"

Boone looked at Windridge. His flushed face also seemed mesmerized, but like a beast, waiting to pounce on his quarry.

Reynolds replied, "*Ich bin der Eigentümer der Glockenspiel Oil Company von München. Das ist mein Personal Die pathetisch-One suchen mit dem Gesicht eines Jackass ist mein Chauffeur der stattliche Germanischen eine mit blondem Haar blaue Augen ist mein persönlicher Leibwächter die kürzere Herren mit dem Asinine Gesicht, meine Familie war freundlich genug, ihn zu nehmen leider ist er Leere der intelligente Unterhaltung das ist der Grund, warum Er dimwitted. Also machten sie ihn zu meinem persönlichen Diener,*" said, a very straight-faced Reynolds.

Then Valentina interpreted this to Major Mo "私はミュンヘンのグロッケンシュピール石油会社の所有者　は私のスタッフ

ですよ！ジャッカスの顔をして *1*を哀れに見える 私の運転手 ブロンドの髪を持つハンサムなゲルマン*1* 青い目 私の個人的 なボディーガード 愚か顔と短い紳士は 私の家族で親切に彼 を取るために何 残念ながら 彼は）」彼は*dimwitted*だ理由で したが インテリジェントな会話の空隙であります."

Major Mo and Capt. Kato left as quickly as they appeared. Dr. von Haag quickly said this to Lt. Boone as he was rubbing his hands over his face.

"This is what dahling Chris just said to that disgusting pig: *I'm the owner of the Glockenspiel Oil Company of Munich Germany. This is my staff! The pathetic-looking one with the face of a jackass is my chauffeur. The handsome Germanic one with blond hair, blue eyes, of course Darling, he is talking about you, Mr. Boone. You are his personal bodyguard. The shorter gentlemen with the asinine face, my family was kind enough to take him in. Unfortunately, he is void of intelligent conversation, completely dimwitted. So, they made him my personal valet!*" Gunny slowly turned his head toward Dr. von Haag.

***

"We had a run-in with him on board ship. It is true the USS Panay was sunk and were there casualties? I think Major Mo is a schmo. He was lying about our ship, *the Panay*, not being marked," said a slightly exasperated Doc.

"Mr. Boone," said Mr. Rabe. "I have an update for you, but I would like to speak you in private," said a concerned Mr. Rabe. Then all eyes centered on Gunny and Herr Reynolds.

Gunny said, "Son, I've seen some knucklehead moves in my career. Enlisted crashing admirals party with their debutante daughters being taken away like Sabine women in the old Roman days. I've seen, Marines with Medals of Honor get drunk having a bad night and spend night in the brig. I have done everything I can in the Marine Corps.—honor, fidelity, Semper Fi, always faithful, but NO, I get you two ball lickers," said slightly more agitated Gunny.

"Is this it? This is how my career is going to end? Babysitting Laurel and Hardy? No, No, God. No, I'm babysitting a big pile of whale shit. Mo, and his eunuch brother, Larry, and wrapped around my two fucking fingers, is Curly," blurted Windridge. "Capital punishment, is way too good for you two, way too fast."

"Gunny is mad as a half-castrated bull, with all due respect," mumbled Hook. "I'm, innocent on this one!"

"Shut the fuck up and snap to, par-don ladies, for my French," said Windridge.

"Given any minute, Hook, you would have gone jabbering, too!" said Gunny. "I'm starting to figure this out. All that jabbering, all these years; you two rat tail fuckers were spawned in some gutter in Pittsburgh. Grew to a certain age, then you two came to my beloved Marine Corps. You could have made life miserable on a worthless Platoon Sergeant in the Army or some bilge sucking Chief Petty Officer, or why don't you two just die in a midair collision like two Navy hot-shot pilots playing chicken. But no, you two are a rancid boil, on each cheek of my ass. Those rancid boils need to be lanced, then to cover that wound, I will have your names tattooed on the cheeks of my ass, putting them on upside down. That way when I turn around, I'll, always see a couple assholes," said Gunny.

Following on noticeably quiet, "You're trying to fuck, my career," whispered Windridge as he ran his fingers through his hair. "I wake up at 4 AM, and at 5 AM I stand in front of my platoon, just to hear the First Sgt. call your name repeatedly, and you're not there. Then you're AWOL, to be shot on sight for going over the hill a deserter. I would win the Navy Cross, what luck that would be. I should have realized that the first time I slung your sorry ass out of the Navy brig, for drunk and disorderly."

"I'm not disorderly, I'm drunk," said Reynolds.

"I told you, Dahling—fine German brandy," said Dr. von Hagg. "Dickey, I found a buffalo-head nickel on my dresser. Christopher, all I found was a penny and half-smoked cigarette."

Hook brushed away his famous mustache with his thumb and forefinger of his right hand, smirking at Dr. von Hagg.

Dr. Hilda listening intently to the interchange. She pulled out a cigarette and handed the lighter to Boone who sparked the roller to ignite the flame. Dr. Hilda and Boone locked eyes as she took a long drag and blew a smoke ring just above his head, flicking her pinkie nail.

"You're not drunk, you're the epitome of stupidity, earning another six months of cleaning the shitters," barked Windridge with unbridled fury. "I'm not done by a long shot! Wherever we go, I'll, find something to make your life sooo fucking miserable boot. My teeth will rot out eating your asses out," said Windridge as he stomped on the toes of Hook and Reynolds, who grimaced.

"Lt. Boone," said Mr. Rabe. "I have grievous news. This is Miss Minnie Vautrin, she is the President of Ginling college. She needs to explain a distressing situation."

"Around 2 AM, a 12-year-old child knocked on my door saying her mom and sisters were hurt and needed medical help immediately. So I quietly knocked on Dr. Lee's door. She got dressed and so did the other doctor, who took their bags and followed the child," said Miss Vautrin with a very sickening look on her face. Then five minutes ago I was handed this envelope. Valentina, could you please read the note."

Valentina opened the envelope and read. "*I have the White Butterfly and the Chinese doctor, too. We are going away and you will never find us*," said Valentina .

Doc looked right at Boone, and said, "Oh my God! She's been kidnapped with Sue."

Dr. Katie buried her face in the chest of Windridge, catching him by surprise, and slowly putting his arms around Dr. Katie to comfort her.

Reynolds said, "So, when I was jabbering, Major Compost had already taken Dr. Brown and Dr. Lee."

"Those sneaky bastards," said Hook.

"What do you want to do, Skipper?" Windridge asked Boone.

"We have to go after her; we must leave now," said Doc with trepidation, as machine-gun fire rattled nearby.

"Sir, at best, they have a five-hour head start on us," said Windridge.

"Mr. Rabe," said Boone. "Sir, you need inform the Japanese military that one of their personnel kidnapped two female doctors, one an American. See, if they can get the two doctors back," he ordered.

"Mr. Rabe, we just got word that Doctors Brown and Lee were put in the back of a Japanese military truck and were heading north by northwest. That was about five hours ago," said Valentina .

"We're leaving very shortly," said Boone.

"What about Betty and Sue? You're sure to follow," said Doc. With tears rolling down her face and her hand trembling as she raised a cigarette to her lips.

"Doc, I know this is a tough one," said Boone. "I'm going to rely on Mr. Rabe and others to get the other two ladies back."

"Oh God," said Mr. Rabe as the door opened and the slight figure of a man in a monk's robe entered the room and approached Mr. Rabe. Rabe turned to the man and shook his hand, then turned to Boone and said, "This is Rev. Black, from the Better Faith than Your Church."

Mr. Rabe reached into the pocket of his coat and pulled out an envelope. He handed the envelope to Rev. Black and said, "Rev. Black, is this a donation given by a member of your flock, *Mr. X*." Mr. Rabe extended his handshake again, and put his hand on the Reverend's shoulder. "Good luck."

Mr. Rabe turned to address the group, "Boone, Doc, and Reverend, I must leave now and contact the Japanese military. God speed."

Reverend Black turned to the group and paused for a moment, then, "Ladies and Gentlemen, I just barely got through. The Japanese Army is starting to lay waste to Nanjing. I happen to be going that way needing to find new flock members along the old ancient Silk Road. I could use the company, and you four gentlemen look like you can fend off the wolves," said the Rev. Black smiling at the four Marines. "And I am sure the Japanese authorities will locate your two Dr. friends. They will be in our prayers tonight," said Rev. Black.

"Ladies and Gentlemen, let's get our cards on the table," said Lt. Boone. "Our orders were to take five ladies, plus Valentina, and get them to a safe location. So much for best laid plans," said Boone, who let out a deep sigh.

"We need to go over the map with everybody," said Rev. Black. "We'll leave Nanjing, by bus traveling up to, Xi' which is over

600 miles away. From Xi' you will take a camel train to your final destination, Kashgar, China," said Rev. Black. "This is about a yearlong trip going west," said Rev. Black.

Silence.

One could hear a cotton ball hit the sand.

Boone broke the silence, "I'm, sure the Japanese officials will get this all straightened out." The girls wiped the tears away from their eyes.

Dr. Katie put her arm around Doc's shoulders and pulled her close, whispering, *"Mé Tá agam Á, Mé Dúilmhear faoistin chuig Scaraire, A cheannsan Croí.* That means *I have a wishful Confession to cut out Major Mo's heart."* Dr. Katie kissed Doc's forehead and said, "It will be alright, my dear friend."

Windridge looked at Dr. Katie who was facing Doc. A small smile cracked his lips as he watched the ladies.

"I take it you ladies have figured out we don't work for the Glockenspiel oil company of Germany," said Lt. Boone. Boone nodded toward Reynolds, frowning. "We're in the United States Marine Corps. We are getting out of here by heading West, according to Rev. Black."

Reynolds spoke to Hook, "Now you can report this the next time we have formation. When Top calls out your name you'll answer to Sgt. Peeping Tom, I squat to piss and I dry humped a camel, Dick Watson Hook, USMC, present," said Reynolds. with a gregarious smile on his face.

"Wipe that piece of shit smile off your face, turd boy," snapped off Windridge, with Reynolds quickly obeying.

"We're leaving in one hour. Make sure you have everything; it's going to be a long, rough ride," reiterated Boone.

Dr. von Haag looked at Reynolds and Hook, and said, "Dahlings, I need to repack my steamer trunks. If you gentlemen could please help for about 15 minutes" Dr. von Haag pointed to the trunks and gestured to Reynolds and Hook to follow her.

Windridge politely, but sarcastically, addressed Dr. von Haag and the two men, "Par-don me, Dahling, but I need my two Dahlings. They need to be with me, Dahling. If you'll excuse us, Dahling ma'am, my two Dahlings and I have work to do, Dahling," said a hard-bitten Windridge in his West Texas twang.

Hook mumbled to Reynolds, "She would've, had 14 minutes of my Wienerschnitzel," as he poked up his campaign hat and scratched his head. "You desert boy. You're like a bad soufflé, seven seconds up, one second down," said Hook as he wiped his famous mustache.

Lt. Boone walked up to the four, and said, "The Glockenspiel Oil Company of Germany? What kind of malarkey was that?" said Lt. Boone.

"Sir, without my quick, sagacious mind in the course of action I took, that goat-smelling asshole, Sir, he would still be poking around and might have found our gear," said a rather proud Reynolds.

"In all these years of your jabbering you did something half-ass right," said Windridge, who slapped Reynolds on the shoulder and pinched Hook on the ear. "I knew it, I knew it, you're a God damn mad Marine genius like your hermaphrodite brother standing next to you! You almost had me. You two rotten fuckers, par-don my French ladies, you two shitheads should apply for Officer Naval School. You could have been straight A-hole+ students if you would have sewn your asshole shut along with your mouth. Within a year, you'd have been a God damn Adm. of Stink pack," said Windridge, vexed.

"And gentlemen," said Windridge as he removed his cover and ran his fingers through his greasy hair. "Think of two words—camel maintenance?" Windridge walked away, and released a ridiculously hard and callous laugh.

Ordinance rained down around the compound, and the crack of rifles was broken by the sharp piercing screams of women being raped and murdered.

Lt. Boone stood silently listening and watching the plumes of smoke rise up throughout the city. He turned and said, "Reynolds, since you're the ad litem executive director of the Glockenspiel Oil Company of Germany, your chauffeur, Mr. Hook, will be driving the bus with you right up front! And to navigate if we run into trouble, I'll have Miss Brandt come up and interpret," said Lt. Boone. "I'll be in the back of the bus being the good-looking bodyguard that I am. I'll have the valet dimwitted one with me back here, too, with the ladies." Sgt. Windridge just grunted.

"Rev. Black," said Reynolds. "What kind of bus is this?"

"It's, a modified German-made, Opel blitz Bus, six-cylinder, five on the floor, with reverse. It's about 28-feet long," said Rev. Black. adding, "As you can see, they've taken out the glass windows, replaced them with metal panels with ports. The main bus door has a slit in it, like those ungodly vile gin joints during prohibition in the states. I have a jail door, then a wooden door between the driver's compartment, and back there is where I kneel to pray, meditate, and rest, there are some bunks back there," said Rev. Black, gesturing to the back of the bus.

"That's real swell, Padre," said Reynolds.

"I'm glad you approve, my blessed son," said Rev. Black.

***

"By the way, Mr. Boone, what are we hauling in this jalopy? Is it road worthy?" Doc lit a cigarette and flicked her nails.

"Well ma'am, we're hauling your gear, our gear, two large crates of Bibles for Rev. Black. There is more gear in the second truck, the third truck, fourth truck. There's extra fuel, food, water, and other gear. Also Rev. Black suggested we don't stop for anything until we get out of town," said Boone as machine guns, rifle blasts, screams and the smell of death permeated the evening air.

"I'm sure the United States Marine Corps can handle whatever comes our way," said Dr. Katie, looking at Wincridge, who just grunted and shook his head.

"Well, ladies and gentlemen, looks like Rev. Black is ready to go and has gotten flags for the bus, trucks, plus his sedan! There is also a roadmap in the glovebox. Sgt. Hook, get me the map, please."

Hook reaches into the glovebox and retrieves the map, then hands it to Boone.

"We have five stops to get to Xi'an," said Capt. Boone.

CHAPTER 13 - BUTCHERED BABIES

Are you driving first, or am I?" asked Reynolds.

"Age before beauty," said Hook, as the bus came to life. Reynolds attempted to put it in first, but there was a high-pitched gear grinding.

"Are you two done fucking around in there? Get us going," snapped Windridge as more grinding gears could be heard. "Par-Don ladies," a slight scowl spread across his face.

"Push the clutch all the way down, numb nuts! Then push the gear shifter up into gear," said Hook.

Reynolds grasped the gear shift and pressed the clutch as far as his feet could reach. He pushes the stick into gear, with metal screaming.

"See what it says?" Hook said as he pointed his middle finger at Reynolds who quickly swatted his hand.

Reynolds shouted, "Fucker! I can't get this clutch all the way to the floor."

Hook instructed, "Dick, slowly release the clutch and don't...." The engine shuttered and died.

"Par-Don Miss Reynolds. When is the last time you drove?" said Hook with wide eyes.

"Suck my dick, Hook. I haven't driven since I got kicked overseas," said Reynolds.

"One more time, Orville and Wilbur Head," said Windridge very sarcastically.

"I think I have this now," said Reynolds. He restarted the engine, stretched his leg out straight to get the clutch to the floor, and pushed the gear shift in place. Reynolds slowly released the clutch and pressed the gas pedal, as the bus moved forward.

Windridge said, "Finally, dickless. My old granny drives better than you."

The convoy pulled out of the safe zone, heavy with gear and leaving a trail of dirt from the dry road.

As they made their way through the Ginling college area, they went through the gate. Rev. Black, with Valentina in the sedan, the two supply trucks and a sedan with four gentlemen in multicolored robes. They took a left at Ninghai Road. Before long, they started to see the carnage as they left Nanjing.

"Chris, are you seeing this shit," said Hook, furious.

"Look, at that motherfucker, Chris, there's another one. With a baby on the end of his bayonet," Hook looked out the window of the bus.

"I can't look at that, brother! The good Rev. Black thinks he's in the Indy 500, and I'm trying to avoid the injured and bodies in the road, along with the Japs," said Reynolds, bouncing in the driver's seat as he looked in every direction. "Fuck this, Tom, watch this!"

"Why what are you going to do," replied Hook. The bus bumped, as Hook saw a Japanese soldier flying in slow motion asshole over elbows, and then smashing into a car, limp. The soldier crumpled to the ground, dead.

"Oops! Some fuckhead jap got lazy in the daisy patch, now he's dead, Fred," shouted Reynolds.

Two bangs rattled the door, and then a voice demanded, "Sgt. Reynolds, you no-driving piece of shit! What did you just hit," asked Gunny.

"A Jap soldier who stepped in front of the bus. His fault the whole way, Gunnery Sergeant!" said Reynolds. Reynolds and Hook shrugged and looked at their faces shit eating grins.

"Outstanding work Sgt. Carry-on with your duties," replied Windridge.

"Lt. Boone, you know someone's going to be asking about that soldier," said Windridge.

"All I can say is, let's get the hell out of here," commanded Boone.

"Lt. Boone, Sir, were coming up on the bridge," said Reynolds.

Lt. Boone watched Rev. Black's car as it reached the bridge and got through. Fires were burning along the bridge illuminating Rev. Black and Valentina's faces.

As the vehicles trundled north, Reynolds and Hook cracked open their soot-covered windows just wide enough to see squads of Japanese soldiers beheading men and boys and lining up the heads along the road. The mutilated bodies were piled with limbs and torsos of various sizes. Through the windows, the men sat horrified as they saw Japanese soldiers running with babies on the end of their bayonets or laying on the road with their heads bashed in. Other soldiers were chasing women and girls stripped naked and running in all directions to try to avoid being ganged raped to death.

As the vehicles rounded a turn, their headlights illuminated silhouettes of men with rifles and machine guns, vehicles parked along the road in a V-shape, pinching the width of the road to allow a single vehicle to pass at a time. Fires blazed from 55-gallon drums at the edge of the road, with orange-tinted smoke rising.

"Valentina, be ready to translate. My Japanese is a little weak."

"A little weak? Instead of playing with your friends, maybe you should have been studying Japanese."

Rev. Black's pulled his car up to the barrier, the bus pulled in behind and then the trucks stopped along the side of the road. Rev. Black stepped out of the car and walked up to the roadblock lined with soldiers with weapons drawn. An officer and an NCO approached. Rev. Black asked, "Do you speak English?"

"Yes, my name is Captain Sato, of the Japanese Imperial Army. State your business in traveling this road."

Rev. Black replied, "We are taking Bibles, machine parts and other supplies and equipment to the village." Rev. Black tapped the window and motioned for Valentina to exit the vehicle. "This here is my traveling companion, Valentina."

Captain Sato nods to Valentina, and removes his glasses, wiping it with a handkerchief. He walks around the black sedan and peers into the windows, kicks the tires as if he is looking to buy it, then back to Rev. Black and Valentina. "Where is your manifest, Reverend?"

One mile past the bridge, Rev. Black turned left toward a medium-size village. On the outskirts, Rev. Black pulled off to the side of the road and stopped. He stepped out of his car and walked back to the bus, where he told Lt. Boone, "As the sinners would say, we BSed them. Whatever they said, it must have worked because they are crossing the bridge," said a relieved Lt. Boone. "So, ladies, our first destination is Hefei."

"Son, we have to take a detour. Then we'll catch back up with each other north to Hefei," said Rev. Black as he blessed Boone with the sign of the cross.

Lt. Boone signaled to all the men to exit their vehicles and rally around him.

"Ladies, it's best you stay inside the bus," Reynolds said as he grabbed his weapon, opened the bus door, and stepped onto the road and began running to catch up to Hook. "Tom, get your ass back here!" he yelled chasing after his friend.

Hook grabbed his M1 bayonet. Reynolds followed suit with his bayonet as they ran around the corner into a smoky house to track and dispatch a Japanese soldier who had run into the building with baby skewered on his bayonet. Hook and Reynolds stopped inside the door. A Japanese soldier kneeled on one knee tending a small campfire. Startled, he turned toward the noise. Reynolds killed the Japanese soldier with a swift stroke across his throat.

Hook noticed an open door and entered cautiously. Inside, he found a Japanese soldier raping a young Chinese girl. Her mouth was bound and her hands tied, with her clothing flung over her back as the soldier assaulted her holding on to her hair. Her eyes were tightly shut, lacking any expression.

Nearby, an elderly man and woman lay lifeless in a pool of blood, throats slit, with their eyes wide open and a look of horror frozen on their faces.

Hook grabbed the soldier around the neck and flung him to the floor. He immediately grabbed his weapon and bayonetted the soldier in the ribs, kicking him off with his boot. His next thrust of the bayonet entered the soldier through the scrotum and exited through his rectum as the Japanese soldier screamed in pure agony. The kill shot was a bayonet in the throat and up through his brain.

"Sir, I'm going after Hansel and Gretel!" said Windridge running after Hook and Reynolds and yelling back to the bus, "Ladies! Don't look outside. Stay down!"

Rev. Black and Boone followed Windridge into the building, but they were too late. They saw Reynolds wiping blood off his bayonet with a blanket. One dead Jap lay in the middle what seemed to be medium-size living room, with a small campfire burning, with burnt meat on the end of a stick on the floor.

"God dammit sergeants!" snapped Boone. "What the fuck, are you doing! You better have a good explanation. Report Sgt.," said a very exasperated and highly pissed off Boone.

"Sir, you didn't see what we saw!" said Hook.

Pointing to the dead man by the fire, "Sir, that one there. I put my bayonet in his heart. He had a little baby and was carrying it into the building skewered on his bayonet." Windridge then pointed to the young Chinese girl, still half naked, with wide eyes of shock and dismay. Windridge gave her a blanket to cover her up, as she stood over the bayoneted baby.

"Go in the other room, Sir. Reynolds killed that Jap because he was raping this young girl. It could be her baby sister at the end of that bayonet," said Hook.

"Then, Sir, go into the first bedroom!" Reynolds says as he looked into Lt. Boone's eyes and nodded toward the bedroom. The elderly couple lay in a large pool of blood against the wall. The Japanese soldier lay splayed on the floor like a gutted fish.

Boone looked at Reynolds and Hook and said, "Outstanding work, men."

Hook walked past the scene to clear the adjacent room. He turned said, "Sir, now you better look at this asap, Sir!"

Lt. Boone steps over the dead man and walks across the room to the door of the second bedroom. He stepped back out immediately as white as a ghost. As soon as he turned, he heard the gasps from their traveling companions who were told to stay in the bus.

"Damn it. I told you ladies to stay in the bus," snapped Windridge.

Dr. Katie returned fire, "I don't work for you, Sergeant."

"What is in there?" said Doc walking toward the second bedroom.

"Babies, with their heads bashed in," snapped Boone.

"Sir," said Hook. "They're hell on wheels against women, teenage girls, babies, old women, and unarmed men. I wonder how they would handle one-on-one with Marine cold steel."

"Oh my God!" shrieked Doc from the second bedroom. "What savages! How can a so-called civilized nation be so brutal!"

"Doc," said Dr. von Haag, "I think that girl wants her baby sister, off that dreaded bayonet!" said Dr. von Haag. The young girl was pulling at the baby, trying to get it off the bayonet.

"Sgt. Windridge, could you please help her? asked Dr. Katie

"Yes ma'am, I will," as Sgt. Windridge gently removed the baby from the bayonet and wrapped it in a blanket, gently handing it to the girl, who proceeded to run away.

"Katie, did you see what was missing?" said Doc as she inspected a woman in the second bedroom.

"She's about 60-years-old. She looks like she's been raped to death! Look at the deep cuts from her vagina to her throat. The heart and the kidney are missing. Looks like we can identify what the burned meat was on the fire out front!" said Dr. Katie.

"So, you are telling me that these Japs eat human hearts, livers, kidneys, gizzards, and what not?" asked Reynolds.

Valentina clasped her hand over her mouth and said, "I'm going to be sick."

"Lt. Boone," said Rev. Black. "My four brothers will dispense of the Japanese devils very quickly. Time is of the essence, so we must continue. The clean-up crew will catch up to us when they are done."

"Chris, I stepped in it is time," said Hook.

"What are they going to do? Send you to Marine barracks in D.C. and go clean the Marine Commandant's commode?" said a sympathetic Reynolds. "The only difference is that you saw him first, and like a good leatherneck, you did the right thing, old buddy."

"I just can't get the image of the baby out of my head!" said Hook.

"Thomas, that makes two of us," said Reynolds with distress in his voice as they drove away.

Boone softened his tone and addressed Reynolds and Hook, but also the others who had witnessed the unspeakable brutal carnage, "What you witnessed will close a chapter in your lives, but new ones have just opened. And fellow Marines, your first priority is protection of these ladies, now let's get on with our mission."

CHAPTER 14 NO LIFER JUICE

"It looks like Rev. Black is slowing down, telling us to follow him that way," said Reynolds. They drove in behind a village, at the far end is a cluster of huts, hidden from the road.

"Ladies and gentlemen," said Rev. Black, "Because of the incidents today, we will not have any fires tonight! We will have meager rations—there is some beef jerky and cold cooked rice. Lt. Boone. I suggest your people turn in early tonight, my fellow brothers, we will be on guard on this blessed ground."

Reynolds mumbled to himself, too tired to hear what Rev. Black was preaching. "Nothing like sleeping out in the open stars with that morning hard on specially with a rock stuck up your ass, that nice chill in the air makes you have to piss off that nice hard on in the morning." He yawned, scratched himself, and shivered. He could see his cold breath as he walked around the other side of the house to relieve himself. Then he watched four females, coming out of the bus, stretching for the morning. He quickly turned around grabbing his pants shuffling away.

***

"No lifer juice," grumbled Windridge.

"Did you mumble something, Sgt. Windridge?" said Dr. Katie.

"Ma'am, I mumble no lifer juice! It's what we call in the Marines a cup of hot joe!" said Windridge.

"I know what that means, Gunnery Sgt. Windridge. You're like damn babies wanting their Pablum in the morning to soothe the savage beast in his morning ritual of cigarettes, hot black coffee— the breakfast of warriors and Kings," said Dr. Katie. Windridge looked at her, but did not want to process her information this early in the morning chill.

"Lt. Boone, it's time to move your people out," said Rev. Black.

"Lt. Darling, where is our next destination in this great Odyssey?" said Dr. von Haag.

"A place called Lushan," said Lt. Boone, looking at the map. The buses and the other vehicles, slowly moved out in the early Chinese morning.

"I've seen cut up cadavers, but I cannot get that carnage out of my head. What we witnessed last night. Such brutality," said Doc. lighting her cigarette. "Plus, there's the matter of Betty and Sue, being kidnapped by those deplorable monsters," said Doc. slowly blowing out the smoke of her cigarette flicking her pinky nail.

"*Mein Gott*," exclaimed Dr. von Haag.

"I received this communiqué from my cousin before we left the states. There's no time like the present to read it," said Dr. von Haag as she unfolded the letter and read it to herself. She pulled out her cigarettes, flicked her lighter and set it near the corner of the letter and lit it, holding it for a few seconds rolling it to make sure it burned. She dropped it on the floor of the bus as it turned to ash. She lifted her lighter up and lit her cigarette, stepping on the ashes.

"Curiosity killed the kitty cat, Hilda. So, what gives?" asked Doc.

"It's my cousin, Dr. Josef Mengele, writing to tell me he joined the Nazi party this year and wants me to join him, helping him work on something called the Final Solution. The Nazi party is like a bad party, with bad partygoers; they drink the bad party champagne, wearing bad party dresses. You never want to wear that party dress. When you find the pattern, tear that pattern up. After living in America for one year, I'll take American Democracy and dreams every day," said Dr. von Haag with a faraway look, flicking her nails, taking a long drag and exhaling the smoke. "And whatever the Final Solution is, it sounds hideous and I want no part of it." The convoy moved out at a slow but steady pace northward to their next destination.

***

"Quit flicking my ear; can't you see I'm driving," said Reynolds.

"Buddy boy, I've seen you're driving; you run over Jap soldiers," said Hooky.

"You seen it, every bit his fault! He should have quit chasing that teenage girl. He ran in front of the bus, then he flew with the greatest of ease. I can't say much for his landing," said Reynolds.

Dr. Katie, says in an Irish brogue *"Níl aon mhaith saseanchas nuair atá an anachain déanta."*

Doc replied, "Yes, you're right. *What is done cannot be undone.* Still, I cannot get the thought of Betty and Sue out of my mind. They're out there, alive or worse, or ending up like those Chinese women, brutally raped or possibly having their heart or kidney eaten. Betty's like my kid sister."

Dr. Katie looked across the bench seat as the bus bumped along the 1000-year-old road. Windridge took his hat off and ran his hand through his thick dirty hair as he glared out into the morning sun."So, Sgt. Windridge," said Dr. Katie. "Tell me a little about yourself?"

Windridge, startled out of deep thoughts, turned to face Dr. Quinncannon. Her light blue eyes twinkled and brightened up the dark and hazy bus.

"So, what is your first name Sgt. Windridge?"

Surprised at the question, he mumbled, "Winthorpe, ma'am," in his Texas twang.

"Please speak up, Sgt., me boyo," said Dr. Katie, flashing him a smile and batting her eyes coyly.

"Ma'am, I function better when I have my jot Joe! In the morning," said Windridge.

"Lifer juice. Is that the only thing that makes you function in the morning, Gunnery Sergeant?" said Katie.

"Sorry ma'am, I don't quite follow what you said. My first name is Winthorpe."

"What a manly name. I think It's old English for masculine," said Dr. Katie. "So, what did you do before the Marine Corps."

"Came from around VanHorn, Texas. Quit school young, then punched and branded cattle," said Windridge.

"Did, you hurt your hands punching adorable cattle?" said Dr. Katie with an innocent smile on her face, in a soft delicate Irish voice.

"No, ma'am, I didn't physically punch the cattle," chuckled Windridge.

"Y'all poke and prod the cattle into a pen, then we cut one out at a time, then brand that cow or bull, then turn them loose to graze in the green pastures. Someday, I'm going to have me about 10,000 acre spread," said Windridge rather proudly.

"I'd like to poke and prod at Reynolds and Hook, then have their names tattooed on my ass upside down," said Windridge snickering.

"So, tell me Winthorpe, are four-legged creatures the only thing you have branded?" asked Dr. Katie.

"Ma'am?" asked Windridge, with wide eyes. "Are you asking me if a cow has branded me? No, none has yet to meet my expectations," said Windridge, as he lit his Chesterfield and pulled his foot up and rested it on his knee. He took a long drag and blew smoke rings straight up into the roof of the bus.

"You're a *dána prásach* one, who seems to fancy himself," said Dr. Katie as Windridge narrowed his eyes and looked at her.

"In English, that means you're a *bold and brazen*, one!" said Dr. Katie chuckling. "So, I take it you are the strong, silent type," asked Dr. Katie

"Except when I'm running my foot up two Marines' asses!" said Windridge, nodding his head toward Hook and Reynolds.

***

Boone turned his attention from listening to the banter of Dr. Katie and Withorpe. "Excuse me, Miss Brandt," said Boone to the woman sitting next to him.

"Yes Lt. Boone?"

"Did you get all your father's paperwork taken care of like you wanted to," said Boone.

"Why yes, I did thank you," replied miss Brandt.

"I so wanted to settle here, work for my father, and one day some handsome stranger would come into my life, and I give my father some grandchildren," said Valentina sadly. "Now, I'm heading to Western China. It is strange how some things work out."

***

"Reynolds, there's Rev. Black, looks like he wants us to pull in over here, behind these large buildings," said Hook.

At the front of the bus, Reynolds turned the wheel sharply left, and followed Rev. Black's hand motion to drive past him and came to a stop.

"We must be in or near the Lushan region." Boone thought out loud to no one in particular.

After a few minutes of stretching their legs, Rev. Black entered the bus and said, "We have followers in this general area, they brought in some rice, hot stew, baozi, some dried fruit, coffee and tea." They went in the house to get their food.

First, Sgt. Windridge got a cup of coffee. As it was being poured into the cup, Windridge grabbed it with both hands and inhaled, just the aroma of fresh brewed lifer juice brought him new life! He took his first taste, in almost 2 days.

"Hooky," whispered Reynolds. "Gunny's at the height of ecstasy; look at his left leg quiver," said Reynolds.

"I don't think he's quite hit the height of his ecstasy yet, that's just a cup of hot Joe," replied Hook. "Grab your chow and let's go out to the bus."

Doc grabbed a bowl and a spoon, and dipped out some hot stew. She picked a baozi and some dried fruit. "I'm going to eat by the bus, then I'm going to have a cigarette, who wants to come with?" asked Doc.

"I will, Darling," said Dr. von Haag, taking a scoop of rice and some stew. She smelled the stew and smiled. "That's delightful."

"May I join you ladies at the bus?" Lt. Boone asked, as he balanced a large bowl of rice and stew and three baozi.

"Yes, be our guest."

The group dined in silence, but for the sounds of eating.

"That was some good chow," said Doc.

Dr. von Haag chirped, "I second that."

"I look up at the moon, wondering if Betty and Sue are seeing the same moon... or worse," said Doc as she leaned back and rested her elbow on the fender of the bus. She lit a cigarette and stared in the night sky.

The group finished their meals, as their hosts gathered bowls and cleaned up the area. Windridge lit a cigarette and contemplated the night's trip.

Everyone went off to lay their heads down for a few hours sleep.

***

"Lt. Boone, Sir," said Rev. Black. "Sir, it's Hook and Reynolds."

"Now what did they do?" said Boone.

"Late last night, a handful of bandits tried to sneak into the area, but they didn't sneak back out, Sir. They ran into your two men," said Rev. Black. "Whoever the bandits are, my men are carrying them back out and cleaning up the mess, so we need to expedite this asap."

"Roger that, Sir," said Windridge.

"Thank you, Gunny," said Boone. As the door opened, Boone stepped into the bus and said, "Ladies, we have to get going immediately."

The ladies stopped chatting and turned to look at Boone. "Oh, my goodness," said Valentina.

Everyone sprung into action gathering their belongings and settling into the vehicles. Reynolds jumped into the cab and slid behind the wheel; Hook sat beside him, and said "Let's get going."

Reynolds turned around and pounded on the door, and shouted, "Are we ready to go?"

Boone said, "Move out, Sergeant!"

The engine rumbled to a start and clunked forward away from the coming dawn. The bus followed Rev. Black's sedan, covered with thick grime and dust.

In the back of the bus, Windridge on a bench trying to get comfortable. He rubbed the sleep out of his eyes and tried to straighten his dirty hair and adjusted his campaign hat onto his head. He leaned back and pulled a pack of cigarettes from his chest pocket, struck a match of his scruffy jaw and lit his smoke. He took a long slow drag and held it in for a moment. Then breathed it out of his nose and mouth. He shook his head hard, and growled, "Again, no God damn lifer juice! Fuck, I hate starting my day off cold. Pardon ladies, for my French." Gunny turned around suddenly and was face to face with Dr. Katie.

"I heard it all, you poor baby! No coffee and your little arse gets chafed, Winthorpe. Man up; it could be worse," flirted Dr. Katie.

"Yes, ma'am," as he tipped his campaign hat to her.

Lt. Boone stood up, stepped forward and stuck his head into the cab looking at Reynolds and then Hook. He asked, "What happened last night, boys?"

"The bandits tried walking in as pretty as you please, Sir. It turned into a good old back-alley brawl, Sir," explained Reynolds, keeping his eyes on the road.

"Lt. Boone, I would've dispatched all five bandits, but…" said Hook.

"But there's always a but, in Hooky's case," said Reynolds.

"Sir, I was skillfully and masterfully engaging the enemy with lethal blows taught to me, by the ancient Masters of China, in the art of deadly hand-to-hand mass destruction. Then Sgt. Flatulence gets in the way of my next two opponents," said Hook. He continued, "Sir, Reynolds barely managed to overcome those pathetic, almost incapacitated opponents. You should have seen them, Sir. Those two men were somewhere in their late 90s with arthritis. To be honest with you, Sir, thank God Reynolds ate one of old lard ass Fitzsimmons famous kimchi and bean sandwiches that he sells for a nickel at the mess hall. Needless to say, they were gassed to death, Sir," said Hook, prodding his buddy.

"Son, you're, so full a shit. That is why your eyes are brown. And what is this shit about ancient Chinese mass destruction secrets? That's a new one," said Reynolds.

"Gentlemen, however the score went down, it sounds like you boys handle yourselves like Marines. Keep it up!" said Lt. Boone.

Vanentina walked to the front of the bus where Boone was standing. "Lt. Boone, I need to stop to, uh, powder my nose."

Boone rolled his eyes and said, "Hey Reynolds, pull off the road up here." He turned to the others in the bus and said, "Now would be a good time to relieve yourselves."

The convoy came to an stop, one by one, and everyone exited their vehicles and found a suitable place to relieve themselves. As they finished, they got right back onto the vehicles.

"I'm, driving for a while squid," said Hook, pushing Reynolds away from the wheel.

Once everyone was back in place and accounted for, the convoy started rolling again.

Windridge and Dr. Katie sat on a bench seat across from Boone. Dr. Katie stared out the window at the passing farmland. Windridge turned to Boone and asked, "Skipper, what is the deal with Rev. Black and all his so-called brothers?"

"I've been trying to figure that one out myself Gunny," said Boone.

"Other than Rev. Black, none of them have talked to us, or even acknowledged us except when they give us food. Then all they say is, 'bless you brother or sister,'" said Windridge.

"Maybe, they have a vow of silence," interrupted Dr. Hilda.

"Well, whoever they are," said Windridge. "They look pretty rough to me, like Mercenaries or Ex-military." Windridge stood up and pulled out a cigarette and rested it between his lips. He walks to the front of the bus and squatted onto his haunches next to the driver compartment, taking out a match. "Sgt. Reynolds, please turn your face to the left."

"Yes, Gunny, why?" said Reynolds. Windridge reached his hand through the bars and struck the match off the left side of Reynolds face, and sat back in his seat without saying a word.

"Fuck, Gunny! God damn that hurt!" squawked Reynolds.

"I told you it felt like 1 million bucks," said Hook rubbing his jaw.

Reynolds snapped back, "Both hands on the wheel, douchebag."

"Do you think I'd forgotten about your crap so soon? Oh no. No way, you pieces of prairie dog shit. Me, myself, and I are just getting warmed up," said Windridge. Gunny pulled his campaign hat to the bridge of his nose to hide his smirk.

***

"Quit trying to give me a wet Willy," said Hook.

"Ladies and gentlemen, someone disagreed with last night's rice in their civilian attire," said Windridge as scanned the group. "I'll tell you right now, it wasn't me," he snapped.

"Quick to throw the scent off there, Windy," said Dr. Katie, flashing an ornery smile. "Alright kids, it was me. I don't feel quite womanly, you know—bad gas, toots, squeaks, and bad aftershave," as she had a big chuckle. "By the way, Lt. Boone, where's the next destination?"

"Someplace called Biyang," replied Lt. Boone looking at the map he had stretched across his knees, straining in the dim morning light.

***

"Are we there yet? How long will it be before we get there; my ass is sore!" squawked Reynolds.

Reynolds moved in close to Hook and blew his putrid breath in his face. "Hook, while you're driving, will you roll down your window, please? Then stick your ass out the window. Then politely stick your tongue out just like the old Marine dog that you are," said Reynolds as he unscrewed the knob on the gearshift and slobbered on it, then screwed it back onto the shaft with spit slowly dripping to the floor in a shiny pool.

Hook looked at the slimy mess, beleaguered. "I guess I'll change your name to Bob on the Knob. Now Shit-For-Brains, leave the knob alone, you fucker. That constitutes dog germs."

Reynolds snickered and pulled away from Hook. He looked out the windshield, and said, "There's Rev. Black. He's waving us to pull over there, in behind these other buildings." The bus pulled into a little grove of trees behind the buildings, and the convoy followed.

***

CHAPTER 15 - DITCHES

"Damn, another cold camp," mumbled Windridge.

"Rev. Black just informed me there are to be no fires tonight. He told me this area is heavy with bandits, CPC, so we're enjoying beef jerky and cooked rice for chow," said Windridge as he handed out slices of jerky. "Grab a bowl and get your rice; it's in a pot on the hood of the bus."

"Don't tell me. no fire for your Pablum? So what else gets you going in the morning, and who's the CPC?" asked Dr. Katie.

"There are two factions vying to take over China: the Chinese Communist party, CPC are the bad guys. The other one is the Kuomintang. The KMT are the good guys. Both groups are fighting the Japanese and themselves," said Windridge. Windridge turned his head giving her a glance, and continued, "No, ma'am, there's also Chesterfield cigarettes and occasionally a dozen eggs, half a slab of bacon, and for the crème de la crème Old lard ass Fitzsimmons, shit-on-a-shingle. And, of course, two pots of lifer juice, you know, a cup of hot Joe, in the mess hall, just to get me going."

Windridge sat back and looked at Dr. Katie for a bit, fidgeting, "Ma'am, what would get you going in the morning?"

"Depends on my appetite," said Katie.

"Sgt. Hook, Sgt. Reynolds, did you get the word, no fire tonight," said Gunny.

"Here's your chow. As soon you two are done eating, get the Pioneer tools out. I want you two to dig drainage ditches for the vehicles about 4 to 6 inches deep and about 12 inches wide, ought to do you." Windridge looked up in the sky. "Looks like rain. Have fun boys."

Windridge climbed up the stairs to the bus. Reynolds and Hook walked to the back of the other truck, grabbing the pick, axe and a shovel. They surveyed the area around the vehicles and decided to start at the front of the bus. Hook grabbed the pick and jabbed it into the ground. Reynolds followed with the shovel, scooping the dirt and rock and stacked it alongside the ditch creating a berm.

"I think I'd rather lay like an old mutt just licking my balls in the corner. I would get so much more gratification out of that than digging ditches," said Reynolds through a big wad of jerky. Hook stopped reached into his pocket for a piece of jerky and stuck it in his mouth yanking a piece off with his teeth and put the rest in his pocket.

Reynolds continued chewing and said, "Man, this is wearing out my jaw."

Hook laughed and chided, "Somethin' to shut you up!" The two men resumed digging along the other vehicles to prepare for the coming rain.

About an hour later, huge flashes of lightning, followed by cracks of thunder, wind gusts, and sheets of rain pelted the men as they continued to work on the ditches. "Tommy the turd, my bloomers are good and wet," said Reynolds.

"I am afraid my silk bloomers are, too!" laughed Hook.

***

Inside the bus, the group sat and watched as Reynolds and Hook made their way around the vehicles. "Sgt. Windridge," said Lt. Boone. "How long are you going to keep them out there."

"Yes! Gunnery Sgt., how long," piped in Dr. Katie.

"Why, what year is it?" responded Windridge. Then rifle shots cracked over the lightning, piercing the air, hitting the metal and windows, glancing over the heads of everyone in the bus.

Windridge ordered, "You two knuckleheads get your asses in here now."

Dr. Katie yelled in old Irish over Windridge's shoulder, "*Sibh salach taispeáin bbréagachs, bhur aghaidh chomh mé féadaim, ciceálann bhur arse.*" Windridge turned around, put his right hand on Dr. Katie's face, and pushed her onto the bus floor, right on her arse. Windridge jumped on top of her to provide cover. Reynolds jumped on the bus and grabbed the steering wheel, Hook followed, closing the door behind him.

Rev. Black and his men returned fire as the Reverend motioned to the caravan to get moving. Reynolds hit the foot feed and spun out in the ditch, lurching forward in the saturated ground.

"Rev. Black said there might be bandits or communists," said Hook holding on as the bus rumbled. The rest of the caravan followed suit. They passed Rev. Black, and Hook yelled, "Jesus fucking Christ, Chris, you missed it! That last lightning strike that just went off and lit up the area! I just seen one of Rev. Black's men kill one of the bandits," said Hook excitedly.

Hook stood up at the cab door and shouted, "Lt. Boone, Sir, I would like to report I just seen one of Rev. Black's so-called brothers, dispatch a bandit."

"Thank you, Sgt. Hook," replied Boone. "I think we're clear of the area, everyone."

Dr. Katie sat up and pushed Windridge off of her. "Are ye done trying to save me life?" asked Dr. Katie, standing and straightening her clothes.

"More than done," replied Windridge, crawling up to a bench and sitting down. Dr. Katie sat next to him giving him a glance and meeting his eyes.

One row back, Doc and Boone sat across from each other talking across the narrow aisle.

"So, what gives with Rev. Black's brothers?" asked Doc.

"Do not quite know ma'am, but at our next stop one way or another I am going to find out?" said Boone, shaking his head back and forth. He turned away and looked out the window.

Doc pulled out a cigarette and lit it, took a long draw and blew the smoke through the small slit in her window. She stared out into the darkness.

At the front of the bus, Reynolds joked, "My feet are soaked, along with my civilian clothes."

"I'm sitting here beside you, happy and dry as a clam!" said Hook. "Your point being?"

"Nothing, just a Marine's bitch," replied Reynolds.

"Plus, you smell like a wet doggy," said Hook to Reynolds.

As the little convoy and its personnel left the area under rain and rain of bullets, hostile conditions into new lands and adventures lay ahead.

CHAPTER 16 - NEED A MATCH

"Hey everybody. Our next destination is Nanyang, which is not very far. A little over 60 miles, looks like we're to stay there the night," said Boone, sitting cockeyed on his bench with his legs in the aisle, map across his lap. "I need a light." Two lighters appear and are sparked to life.

"Boone, do you have confidence in this trip?"

"I have confidence of God. We're going the right path to Keishi."

At the front of the bus, "Get that wet finger out of my ear," said Reynolds.

"Are we there yet, I'm bored, I have to go to the head, and I'm hungry. Are we there yet?" Hook whined as he performed hand puppets in front of Reynolds's face.

Reynolds slapped at Hook's hands, annoyed.

Hook laughed, "Two hands on the wheel, jack off!"

***

"You big *Sracadh*," said Dr. Katie.

"Sorry, ma'am, did you say something?" said Windridge.

"I called you a *jerk*," conveyed a frosty Dr. Katie, still reeling from their encounter earlier.

"For what? Saving your life," said Windridge.

"Me life was far from danger, Gunnery Sergeant.. Meself had it under control," snapped back Dr. Katie with a fiery tone.

"Is that why you were hiding behind me?" said Windridge.

"I wasn't hiding. The fact is, that fat pumpkin head of yours got in the way," said Dr. Katie, her eyes baneful of Windridge.

"By the way, ma'am, what did you say earlier to those bandits back there?" asked Windridge, placidly.

"Huh? What? Oh, right. I said, '*Ye dirty bastards, show your face, so I can kick your Arse.*'" Dr. Katie pulled out her compact, looked in the little mirror and said, "Since you have more brawn than Medulla Oblongata," said Dr. Katie, adding, "I should dot your eye. Those big old course hands have managed to smudge my lipstick and rouge. Even out here, a *Bean Dochtúir* has to look her best. By the way, that means*, Dr. Woman*."

"Ma'am, you putting that crap on your face, is like me needing a cup of hot joe at 4:30 AM. So, with all due respect, both you and Mr. Oblongata need to man up and remember it could be worse." He tipped his Campaign hat, turned away and pulled out a Chesterfield, took a stick match out of his front pocket, running his match down his lower right jaw as the match exploded into flame with the smell of sulfur and hair.

"Hook."

"Yes Gunny. Need a match?

"No, no. I'm good Gunny. No thanks," said Hook.

Windridge and Dr. Quinncannon shot hard glances at each other.

"Your Sgt. Windridge. He doesn't talk too much, does he," Doc inquired to Boone.

"I've only been around for about three weeks. I didn't get to meet everybody in the Regiment. This mission was, as they say, thrust upon me," said Boone.

***

"When you were off to college, did you travel to the Rugen island?" Dr. von Haag broke their silence, sitting side by side on the bench. The bus trundled along the bumpy road.

"Why yes, I did," replied Valentina.

"Did you stop at the resorts at Sellin Binz when you where there? Did you see the *Konigsstuhl*, the Kings chair?" said Dr. von Haag.

"Yes, I love the white cliffs," said Valentina.

"How, I miss the decadent desserts! Cheesecake, *Kuchen, Prinzregententorte, Spritzkuchen, streusel, or a Coburger Bratwurst, Bratkatoffeln* with onions and bacon, and a couple bottles of Pilsner," said Dr. von Haag. as she lit her cigarette flicking her pinxy nail.

"Skipper," asked Reynolds, yelling through the bars of the cab door.

"Yes, Sgt.," said Boone.

"Looks like Rev. Black is waving his arms ahead for us to go into a warehouse," said Reynolds.

"Roger that, Sgt. Reynolds," said Boone.

The bus came to a stop inside the warehouse. Rev. Black gestured to open the door, so Hook pulled the handle. Rev. Black stepped onto the bus, looked at everyone, and said, "We're going to spend the night here, brothers and sisters. It's going to rain later on. We'll be out of the rain. We'll be able to make some hot food, bread, and hot coffee," Rev. Black explained.

"Rev. Black," said Lt. Boone.

"Yes, my brother," respondent Rev. Black

"Exactly what kind of religious order, are you in," said Boone.

"Brother, we have taken a vow of silence, we are you in the order, that helps fellow man," replied Rev. Black.

"Rev. Black, one of my sergeants, reported that one of your fellow Brothers whacked a bandit," said Lt. Boone.

"Yes, that would be Brother Gray. The vivid vernacular is quite dissimilar than I am used to, Brother, but if you mean we smite the wicked, then yes! As you say, he whacked a bandit," said Rev. Black.

"I must get back to the Brothers for self-flagellation, then there's maintenance to do on the vehicles," said Rev. Black.

"Hook and Reynolds," said Sgt. Windridge.

"In the Back of the second truck, there is some of our gear, go get it and bring it into the bus," said Windridge.

"Then go change out of your wet diapers," commanded Windridge.

"Thank God," said Reynolds and Hook together.

"I'll, get in the back of the truck, puss boy," said Hook.

"Holy shit Chris, there is just more than our gear? in this truck, we need to get back to the LT. ASAP!" said Hook. as Hook and Reynolds, took their gear into the bus, closing the door.

"Sir, some of the crates that Rev. Black has in the back of his truck, as they say, cracked open Sir, 12 45 Thompson machine-guns, with ammo and clips Sir, tucked away in straw," said Hook.

"Sir, seems to me them old boys Sir, if you ask me Sir, they sound like a bunch of pole cats Sir," said an agitated Windridge.

"Toting Thompsons, instead of toting Bibles and whatever the hell else," said Gunny.

"That's not all, there are four satchels, each with about $25,000 cash in each Sir," said Hook.

"They must have an excellent collection system," said Reynolds. Everyone looked at Reynolds, dumbfounded.

"Sgt. Hook?" said Lt. Boone.

"Yes sir!" reported Hook

"Is all $100,000 dollars, still in that crate Mr. Hook, you Sgt. Reynolds?" said Boone.

"Sir, were Marines, I personally got up in the truck," said Hook.

"Sir! I was a wet puss, at that time Sir," said Reynolds. In kind of a jestfull way.

"Did you get all our gear out of that truck, douche bags?" asked Windridge.

"All are gear, plus these two bags, this small chest that Dr. Kendall picked up at the college," said Reynolds.

"Hundred thousand clams," said Dr. von Hagg.

"I, would tuck it away, finish out my 40 years from my beloved Marine Corps, then buy Mdm. Wang's, house of pleasure," said Reynolds.

"Hook old man, you could buy in, becoming a silent partner Mr. Hook, you could clean out the spittoons, slop the floors clean, do the dishes, but me, the great entrepreneur that I am, I'll, be the new face of the swankiest establishment in Nanjing," said Reynolds as he lit a cigarette.

"All the best crooners, Crosby, Astaire, Rogers, Actors, Actresses, the A1 list from Hollywood, Gable, Powell, Loy, DE Havilland, comedy acts, the real Mo, Larry, and Curly will come here from the US," said Reynolds.

***

"Miss Brandt, I know you're thinking of your father, just by your faraway eyes," said Boone.

"I know it's like to lose a parent, it's never easy! but you have to live your life! even if it means taking a different path in your life! but you cannot hide in a shell, if you let it, it will worsen," said Boone.

CHAPTER 17 - HOT JOE AND A 45

"Lt. Boone Sir, first call," said Windridge.

"What time is it Gunny," asked Boone.

"It's 4:30 AM, Sir; Rev. Black says we have just enough time to chow down, Sir," said Gunny.

"Are the four ladies up?" said Boone.

"Sir, I only saw Dr. von Haag up," relayed Gunny.

"What about Hook and Reynolds? Are they up too?" said Boone as he and Gunny cracked a smile.

"Yes, Sir, I just got Butt-Stroke and Butt-Head out of the rack," said Windridge.

"Roger that, Gunnery Sergeant," said Boone, scratching his head.

"Gunnery Sgt. Windridge," said Dr. Katie, walking to him with a large cup of coffee in her hand. "Did you get your hot coffee, Pablum to soothe the savage King Marine beast?" asked Dr. Katie, grinning.

"Why no, I did not.," said Windridge as he walked toward the coffee pot where the food was being cooked. He picked up a tray and scooped his portion of food. He stepped toward a man standing by the coffee and said, "Excuse me, Padre, what's your name?"

"Brother Black."

"God dammit, par-don Padre, who just got the last cup of coffee?" asked Windridge.

"Please Brother, I'm not used to hearing the Lord's name in vain," said Brother Black as he nodded toward Katie Quinncannon.

Windridge slowly turned his body around and walked by her, quipping, "I thought you threw lipstick on your face, not coffee in mine. I assumed you gave aid and comfort to the Marines."

"You American males, especially with uniforms on. *Griothnairt báb*," sniffed Dr. Katie.

"Par-don Ma'am, I have not a clue what you just said?" said Windridge.

"I just called you a *Grunting baby,*" replied Dr. Katie. "On the coffee, it was early bird gets the worm. Brother Black gave me the last cup of coffee. Me wanted to give it to you with or without the bravado, the chivalry, even though he has his own little idiosyncrasies like hot coffee Pablum in your belly, in the yellow sun of the morning. Me have me own idiosyncrasies! That is what makes the world go around Gunnery, Sgt. me boyo," said a spry Dr. Katie.

"Ma'am, did you just call me yellow belly?" blurted Windridge.

"No, I don't think you have jaundice. Your eyes are grand, even though they are radiant blue-green color, but we must have more of an private setting to see if you are a yellow belly! You'd have to take your blouse off, but by my observation, you do not wear an undershirt," said Dr. Katie. She stopped and calculated, "I, I, mean you are brave, and you put yourself above others, just like that little action you performed earlier," said Dr. Katie.

"Well ma'am, I do apologize, and I do appreciate the hot cup of joe," said Windridge, tipping his campaign hat her way. He looked down at cup of coffee in Dr. Katie's hands and reached out to take it. "Cold," he said.

***

"Lt. Boone," said Reynolds leaning back from the cab.

"Yes, Sgt. Reynolds," replied Boone.

"Rev. Black is ready to go," said Reynolds.

"Roger that, Sgt."

As the convoy left Nanyang to head to their next destination, Sgt. Windridge was the last to board the bus. He looked down at Hook, holding two cups of steaming hot lifer juice. Windridge looked at his large cup of cold coffee and took a swig. He shuddered, sat down and said, "Skipper, where are we heading?"

"A place called Shangluo, about 180 miles," said Boone.

"Would you look at that, Winthorpe? Your coffee is cold, even with your hot wind," said Dr. Katie.

Windridge looked at her, then back at his cold cup of lifer juice.

Hook mumbled to Reynolds, snickering, "She called him Winthorpe!"

The door between the driver's compartment and the rest of the bus opened. Gunny ordered, "Sgt. Reynolds, please throw this cold crap out." Windridge handed his cup to Reynolds, who emptied the cup through the bus door. "Thank you, Sunshine. Now empty both of your cups in that one, ASAP."

Hook looked up with shock and surprise, but without saying a word, emptied the hot coffee into Windridge's cup and handed it back to Windridge.

"Thank you, kindly boys," said Gunny, as both doors closed.

"Never been held up with the 45," said Reynolds to his buddy Hook.

"What happened to the bravado, chivalry, and not a 45, I witnessed not too long ago," said Katie Quinncannon, as she glared at Windridge.

"Ma'am, I'll let you know after I finish this cup of hot joe," as he pulled out a Chesterfield and a stick match, striking it downward with his thumbnail, igniting the match lighting his cigarette, with a few cracks of his wrist putting out the flame. Then taking a slow extraction of lifer juice, as hot coffee went down his throat, hot smoke came on his nose.

"Darling Doc. There's still an issue. We are all still saddened about Betty and Sue," said Dr. von Haag.

"I can't get that out of my mind; are they dead? Are they lying in the middle of the road somewhere naked? Are they buried in an unmarked grave with part of their guts gone, eaten by the Japanese?" agonized Doc. "This is driving me crazy," said Doc, wiping tears from her eyes.

"The roads are still very packed with human traffic heading north, away from the fighting," said Valentina to Lt. Boone.

"Losing one's home from war or natural disaster is nothing but dire straits, especially if you've lived there all your life and you have nowhere else to go. No help," said Valentina. "With the life that I decided to accept, I know living in one place would be a fleeting thought, with moving all the time from post to post is hard on the family."

***

"God, my ass is sore. I've not done this much driving since before I joined Marine Corps," said Reynolds, adding, "Back home I would just steal a jalopy, then I would just drop it off, then do my business, then just take another one. Of course, it only takes one time to be caught and sent to the big house where they make you a butt puppet, or sent to the Marine Corps. The only difference is we work for Uncle Sam; so here I am, now a sergeant in the Marine Corps., driving north by bus," said Reynolds.

Reynolds stared at the road ahead of him and shifted his butt back and forth. He continued, "Then we would jump on a camel, head to Western China for almost a full year… what else is a Marine to do, other than war," said Reynolds.

"Being upstairs at Mdm. Wang's in my dress blues waiting for Christmas morning to open my present," replied Hook.

"Where's your sense of adventure," countered Reynolds.

"Puss boy, again upstairs waiting to open up my present," said Hook as he rolled his eyes at Reynolds.

"Aren't you Ebenezer Scrooge," said Reynolds.

"Why, yes I am! Especially when I have to pay for it," as they both chuckled.

Reynolds spotted Rev. Black ahead, waving at them and pointing to the left.

"Lt. Boone," yelled Reynolds to the back of the bus. "Rev. Black, is asking us to turn in here."

"Roger that Sgt," Boone shouted back.

The bus rolled to a stop, with the caravan rolled past the bus as ground guys pointed the way to park.

Rev. Black stepped onto the bus, opened the two doors from the cab into the back and stood in the doorway. He looked around and said, "Lt. Boone, we just got word that our next destination is in a major fight in the middle of the city. The communist nationalists are fighting, so were going to stop, refuel here. Anybody needs to relieve themselves, do it now because we are on a mission from God and we only have about 10 minutes," said a hurried Rev. Black.

Everyone filed off the bus to find a place to relieve themselves. As they returned to the bus and their positions, Reynolds looked around. "Where is Hooky?" he asked.

"By my time, he's 30 seconds late," said Windridge.

"There he is," said Reynolds pointing toward the buildings surrounded by woods. "Let's go, Richard; the principal and staff want to go and go now," said Reynolds.

"Don't feel so good," Hook mumbled.

"Daniel Boone, did you try take a shit in the woods like a bear," said Reynolds.

"No, but I got shit on," as Hook fell into his friend, Reynolds, with a knife sticking out of his back.

"Oh fuck!" Reynolds said, "What happened to you buddy?"

"Get him in here and put him on his stomach on the bed in the back. Be careful about that knife; we don't want it moving," Doc ordered, adding "Sgt. Reynolds."

"Yes, ma'am," replied Reynolds, as he guided his friend to the back of the bus and gently laying him face down on the bed. "I got your back, buddy. There you go, Doc. He's all yours."

"Get this piece of shit bus out of here now, Son. And try to keep it smooth," commanded Doc.

"Roger that, Skipper," said a surprised Reynolds as she administered orders. The bus was rambling away. Doc, Dr. Katie, and Dr. von Haag were around Hook on the bed.

"Katie, hand me my bag, please," said Doc, calmly. "We must be incredibly careful to extract that knife from his Infraspinatus Fossa. Hold him down," said Doc.

"What did you just say ma'am?" asked Windridge.

"It's called the scapula," said Doc.

"Come again," said Windridge as he yanked the knife out of Hook's back.

"It's called the shoulder blade, you dunderhead," said Dr. Katie.

"I have clean bandages in my bag," as Dr. von Haag. She went into the bag to get the bandages.

"Keep direct pressure on that open wound," said Doc.

Dr. Katie and Windridge applied direct pressure with their hands on top of each other.

"Fuck, that hurts," mumbled Hook.

"I bet it does, stud," replied Doc.

"Good, I hope it gets infected, and they have to drain the pus every day," said a spiteful Windridge.

"So, how did this happen, Sgt.," asked Doc.

Hook mumbled, "Got there, did my business, turned around and took about three paces, and that bit my back," mumbled Hook.

"Dr. Katie, can you assist, please," said Doc.

"I'm right here, Doc," replied Dr. Katie back calmly.

"We have no hot water, but he still needs to be cleaned around the area," said Dr. von Haag.

"Gunnery Sgt., right now, your arse is in the way. Please go sit up front with Sgt. Reynolds and antagonize him," ordered Dr. Quinncannon.

"Lt. Boone," yelled Reynolds. "Rev. Black is signaling us to stop ahead." The bus came to a stop.

Rev. Black told Doc. "Dr., there's medicinal liquor and a medical bag in a little compartment on the right-hand side of the bed,"

Dr. Katie pulled out a bottle from a brown paper bag, and said, "Bush Mills, a bottle of Bush Mills. How marvelous," said Dr. Katie. She cracked the bottle open and took a pull from it.

"Hooky," said Dr. Katie. "This liquor is way too grand to be poured on an open wound like that," as she chuckled. Then she helped Hook to his side so he could take a big drink. She took the bottle away from his lips and poured about two seconds of liquor on his back as he cringed.

"Damn ladies, that hurt," said Hook.

"Hush, Puss boy," said Dr. Katie. Doc and Dr. von Haag tended the wound.

"Here, Darling Tom," said Hilda, as she put a lit cigarette to his lips.

"Valentina, could you help him with his cigarette, please," said Hilda von Haag.

"Anything to help," replied Valentina as they switched positions by Hook.

"Doc, wash your hands with this Bush Mills," said Dr. Katie. Doc stuck her hands out and Dr. Katie's dashed her hands with Bush Mills, as she rubbed her hands together and shook them off to dry.

"Woman, take a snort," said Dr. Katie to Doc. Dr. Katie fed her a little drink, gave herself one, and then turned it over to Dr. von Haag, who took her snort and then held up Hook's head.

"Darling, looks like you're done with your cigarette," said Dr. von Haag, nodding to Valentina, who took the cigarette from Hook's lips and snubbed it out with her foot on the bus floor. Dr. von Haag helped him take a big drink of Bush Mills. Then Doc poured the liquor on his open wound again.

Doc opened the medical bag and found a needle and thread. She measured out enough to suture the 3-inch gash. She inspected the wound to see how much damage had been done and decide where to put the stitches. Doc carefully started to suture Hook's shoulder blade between bounces of the bus. Dr. Katie kneeled in between Hook and Doc to steady herself and continued applying pressure, moving her hand each time Doc gave her a nod. Dr. von Haag stood behind Doc and shined a flashlight on the wound. Hook winced with each pinch of the needle; even Bush Mills couldn't suppress the pain.

Doc dabbed the area to clean it as much as possible, and said, "Katie, I think that's as good as it's going to get for now." She turned to face Hook and looked him in the eye, "Now, that is done, there's 22 skidoo," said Doc.

"Thank you, Doc," mumbled Hook.

"Sgt. Hook," Doc said as she lit a cigarette. "Is Thank you all your payment? Anyway I don't think you can afford my prices. That's $1,000 dollars a stitch. You owe me $22,000 clams. How are you going to pay for that surgery. Do you have insurance?" said Doc, with a very straight face. She broke into a broad smile and laughed,"I'm pulling a fast one Hooky. I'm not a gold-digger kiddo—that is Hilda."

Dr. Katie got up to change positions and said "Ladies, there is three rolls of gauze in the medical bag. Let me bandage him up."

***

"What the fuck happened out there," demanded Gunny, leaning up against the door to the cab.

"I don't know, Gunny," said Reynolds.

"Where were you?" asked Gunny.

"I took a quick piss and came back," said Reynolds.

"Dumbshit, you know better! You go in buddy pairs; do you Roger that Sgt. Maggot Shit?" said Gunny, in his hard Western Texas twang.

"Roger that, Gunnery Sergeant," said Reynolds.

Windridge walked to the back of the bus and asked, "How's Numbskull?"

"No, worse for the wear, and no thanks to you, numbskull," declared Dr. Katie matter-of-factly.

Gunny was taken aback at her statement. He walked back to the cab, opened the door and sat down in Hook's seat.

"Gunny," Reynolds said quietly. "May I speak frankly, Winthorpe?"

Gunny slowly turned his head toward Reynolds with wide eyes. "This one time, you can spill your malarchy with me," whispered a poker-faced Windridge.

"Well, Winthorpe, I think Dr. Katie, is quite the live wire for you, Winthorpe. Plus, in your own way, you're kinda handsome Winthorpe, which would make her quite a catch for you, Winthorpe; also, don't forget she's a riot; at your wedding reception, the two of you make a handsome couple! You're out there, cutting a rug Winthorpe," said Reynolds. "Winthorpe, you've already shown in her eyes that you're brave in a cruel, unusual, harsh way, but you're not diddly shit or squat, or is it squat to diddly shit, nor are you a lamebrain, twit, and far from a drip, maybe a little on edge, maybe some pent-up anger issues, but not too far from being certifiable, Winthorpe? Nothing but a stiff drink, a good woman, a stiffy, and another stiff drink with your buddies to talk about it. You know, Sergeant's time."

Reynolds gave Gunny a little shot to the arm and a wink to the eye. "She has Irish eyes for you, Winthorpe. If I was you, I would play hardball, Winthorpe. You two can throw a little shingle up. You've been looking to retire from the Marine Corps, Winthorpe. Then you can have little Winthorpes, Winthorpe!"

Reynolds continued to look straight ahead, a big smile on his face, with both hands on the wheel. A quick, excruciating pain scraped across the right cheek of Reynold's face. A heavy volume of smoke rings hit one after another, causing Reynolds to cough. He whispered, "Fuck Gunny, thanks again for sharing a butt, Winthorpe."

Gunny turned opposite to Reynolds in his seat, quickly seizing Reynolds by the throat with his right hand and whispering in his ear, "Dick, the name is Gunnery Sgt. Windridge, United States Marine Corps."

Reynolds face turned beet red as he was gasping for air. Windridge let go, and Reynolds bull-frogged this out, "Alrighty, Roger that (cough) Gunnery Sgt. (cough) Windridge," pulling at his collar. Suddenly another cannonade of smoke hit Reynolds followed by another solvo of smoke.

"A little touchy aren't we Gunnery Sgt. Windridge," said Reynolds as another sweep of smoke peppered his face. Gunnery Sgt. Windridge whispered, "Do you think she real sweet on me?"

"Like a fully operational water cooled dirty 30 caliber machine gun," whispered Reynolds rubbing his red throat. He rolled down his window, halfway waiting for the next volley of smoke.

"Like, like she wants to get hitched and have youngins?" whispered Gunny, surprising himself.

Reynolds whispered, "At least it's not a shotgun wedding."

Gunny answers back, "I don't think I could retire from the Marines quite yet! I'm still pretty young; I have to get the skipper's permission. Why in the fuck am I talking to you about this you shithead boot," Windridge chastised Reynolds.

***

"Katie," whispered Doc in the back of the bus.

"You're hitting Sgt. Windridge pretty hard, you know, kinda thick—don't you think?" said Doc.

"Like whale blubber that's kindly between his ears." Dr. Katie. said

"He, so damn handsome. Yes, I would like to see under that shirt and more," whispered Dr. Katie seductively licking her lips. The four girls chuckled.

"How are you doing, Sgt. Hook," said Doc, crouching down and lifting up the dressing to check the wound.

"Hurts like hell, Doc; not only does my back hurt, but I think I just split a gut. I just overheard Dr. Katie talking about Windridge," said Hook.

Dr. Katie moved in close to Hook's ear and said, "So, you be kind of a *caincíneach rósach*." Dr. Katie stood, crossed her arms and looked down at Hook. "If you want to know, what I said, "I said that you are a *Nosy Rosie*," conveyed Dr. Katie. "So, in the meantime, you need to keep your gob shut, lay still, and get some rest. Here, have another drink, Navy," she snickered.

Doc threw a blanket around Hook's neck, making him as comfortable as possible, and turned it over one fold. "That should hold him!" whispered Doc to Katie and Hilda.

***

"Lt. Boone," said Windridge through the door.

"Yes, Gunny," replied Boone, standing and walking toward the front of the bus.

"It looks like Rev. Black wants us to stop," said Windridge.

The bus pulled alongside the black sedan. Rev. Black walked over to the bus and addressed Boone.

"Lt. Boone, 100 yards up this road we're going to pass through a patch of trees. On the other side of that is a stable where our camels are. There's some large outbuildings where we're going to hide the bus, the sedan, and the two trucks," said Rev. Black.

"Lt. Boone," said Windridge through the door.

"Yes, Gunny," replied Boone, standing and walking toward the front of the bus.

"It looks like Rev. Black wants us to stop," said Windridge, nodding toward the black sedan ahead.

The bus pulled alongside the car. Rev. Black stepped out, adjusting his coat, and walked over to address Boone.

"Lt. Boone, 100 yards up this road, we're going to pass through a patch of trees. On the other side is a stable where our camels are waiting. There are large outbuildings where we'll hide the bus, the sedan, and the two trucks," said Rev. Black, his voice low and firm.

Boone gave a slight nod. "Understood."

"Well, here we are," said Dr. von Haag, stretching her arms as she stepped out.

"Lt. Boone," said Doc, her expression serious. "Since we're going to be in a safe, quiet, dry place, I suggest we let Sgt. Hook rest here for at least five to seven days. He needs time to recover before we move again. I trust there are accommodations to take care of our friend?"

Boone ran a hand through his hair. "I fully agree, Doc. Yes, there should be space." He glanced toward Rev. Black. "I'll talk to him about it since he financed this little sojourn."

Rev. Black walked up just as Boone turned to face him.

"Lt. Boone, did you say something about financing this expedition?" asked Rev. Black, tilting his head slightly.

Boone squared his shoulders. "Why, yes, I did. And you know one of my sergeants is wounded in the back of our bus."

"I fully realize that, Lt.," said Rev. Black, his voice clipped. "But we are leaving in the morning. All of us."

"Rev. Black, please reconsider. The doctor says we need at least five to seven days to let Sgt. Hook recover enough to travel," Boone pressed, his stance unwavering.

"I am sure the good doctor has her schedule for her patient," Rev. Black replied, crossing his arms. "But I have my schedule with God. Time is of the essence. So, brothers and sisters, one must be ready to go in the morning."

Boone let out a slow breath, rubbing his chin. "So, this is how it is to be?"

"Brother Boone, if you stay here in the morning, you will miss the caravan," Rev. Black stated. "Do you know your way around the city? I doubt it."

"You need to purchase camels and supplies," Rev. Black added, his gaze unwavering.

Boone inhaled deeply. "Rev. Black, I'd like to confess something that's been bothering me for a while. And I'd like to ask your opinion about it." His voice was calm, almost conversational, as he gestured for the reverend to step aside.

The two men disappeared around the side of the truck.

Two minutes later, Lt. Boone returned, casually rubbing his knuckles. He looked at the group with a smirk.

"Girls, Rev. Black changed his mind! He confessed to me that the best opinion was that we stay here for seven days."

Doc arched an eyebrow. "Any dental denial from the good Rev.?"

"Oh, yes," Boone chuckled. "He gutted it out, too. Couldn't back out of it, what with the doctor's orders and all."

Windridge stepped out of the bus and approached Boone, glancing at his hand. "Sir, what happened to your knuckles?"

"I was picking my nose," Boone deadpanned.

Windridge smirked. "Sir, I see you picked pretty close." They exchanged amused glances.

His expression turning thoughtful, Windridge added, "Something is strange, Sir. Speaking of shaving, I've never seen a religious order have beards."

Boone nodded slightly.

"Skipper," Windridge continued, lowering his voice. "Rev. Black gave us four suitcases—two for us, two for the ladies. Also, Sir, his voice... it's slightly familiar."

Before Boone could respond, Rev. Black reappeared, dabbing at a trail of blood dripping from the left side of his lip.

"Rev. Black," said Boone, his tone measured, "would you like one of our doctors to look at your busted lip?"

Rev. Black shook his head. "No, my dear sister. I will have one of my other brothers tend to it."

Gathering himself, he raised his voice. "Everybody, gather around."

The group shuffled closer, their expressions wary.

"Here's what's going to happen. I'm having you dress as Bedouins—Arabian Bedouins," Rev. Black declared.

Reynolds frowned. "We'll look out of place in China dressed as Bedouins."

Rev. Black smiled knowingly. "No, my blessed son. Many civilizations have traveled the Silk Road for trade into China and back to the West. Alexander the Great, Persia, Greeks, the Roman Empire, Vikings, the Dark Ages, the Crusades, the Mongols, Marco Polo… they all sought the luxurious silken fabrics and rare spices of royalty." He clasped his hands together. "So, they'll think nothing of how you are dressed. They've seen it for thousands of years."

Katie Quinncannon crossed her arms. "So, what kind of garb are we wearing?"

"The men will wear the traditional white *thoab* overgarment with *serwal* pants," Rev. Black explained. "Then you'll put your pistol belt and knife on. Your headgear will be the red and white *shemagh*."

He turned toward the women. "Ladies, you'll be wearing the traditional black *madraga* overgarment. But don't worry, yours is made out of silk, not goatskin. And you will keep your pants on."

Doc huffed. "Well, that's a relief."

Rev. Black lifted a piece of fabric. "You'll cover your heads with a *usaba*, like this." He demonstrated, wrapping it around his head with practiced ease.

The group exchanged looks. It was clear—this mission was about to take on an entirely new shape.

CHAPTER 18 - SORE ASS

"As soon as you change into your clothing, I will introduce you to old Li. He owns and runs a 72-camel caravan," said Rev. Black.

"Lt. Boone," he continued.

"Yes, Rev. Black?" Boone replied.

The caravan watched as Rev. Black bowed and shook hands with a slight man with a white beard and a long white pigtail that reached down to the base of his back. The group began to gather outside of their vehicles, and Rev. Black motioned them closer.

"My brothers and sisters, this is Old Li. He's been running caravans for over 60 years."

The men stepped forward to shake hands with Li, and the women bowed to show their respect.

Everyone collected their assigned clothing and sought a place to change. Hook slowly climbed down the steps, wincing at every movement. Reynolds spotted him exiting the bus and approached him.

"Hey, Shit-for-Brains, I look outstanding in white! Oh, shit, I should throw up 'cuz that means I'm in the Navy. When I'm done in my beloved Marine Corps, I'm going to have some real nice white civilian suits in silk. Yep, I'll buy Mdm. Wang's place. You know, Hooky, my boy, I'm fond of a good chicken wing. So picture this in what little mind you have left—a big sign: *Mdm. Wang's Wings*," Reynolds said, waving his arms in the air to show the size of the sign. "And get this, it will be in neon lights. Thomas, I'll be the class of the place, and son, you'll be the ass of the place," Reynolds snickered.

Windridge walked up to the pair and said, "Hey, you dumb shits?"

"Hooky, Gunny wants to talk to you," said Reynolds as he scratched his not-so-famous mustache.

"No, dumb shit! I want to talk to you, Ball Sack. That was almost a world record for you," said Windridge.

"For what, Gunny?" replied Reynolds.

"For keeping your goddamn mouth shut," said Windridge.

"So I could think about what you said about Rev. Black," Windridge continued, scratching his head.

"Why, you're not trusting the good-souled Rev.?" Reynolds smirked.

"I don't know. The way Padre said 'headgear'—just something fishy about our Rev. friend," said Windridge. "His voice is vaguely familiar, I just can't place it."

***

The Women's Suitcases

"Ladies, let's see what's in the suitcase," said von Haag, as she opened the case and lifted the black *Madraga*. The soft garment flowed down from its folded state and nearly hit the floor. The simple black silk threads shone in the sunlight. It was stunning.

Dr. Katie looked in awe as she touched the fine stitching. She held her *Madraga* up against her slender figure as if to try it on.

"He was right about real silk! This would make a fine wedding dress. The only problem is—it's black," said Dr. Katie.

Dr. Hilda chuckled. "Unless you wanted a macabre wedding, *dahling*," she said, sounding like Marlene Dietrich. "If you're thinking about marrying that Cro-Magnon brute of a man, this would be a perfect color for you, Katie."

The women laughed heartily, then abruptly went silent, each admiring the detailing. It had been weeks since they held clean clothes, and they were giddy with excitement.

"What bridal accessories would you wear with that?" piped in Doc. "White gloves, white purse, white shoes... or red on red on red? At this rate, you'll have your wedding at his funeral."

Dr. Katie chuckled and said, *"Sé be céadfach timpeall aige Éide sheirbhíse ná aige fásach Éadach ná, sé nach bhfuil arú cac faoi a bean."*

"Dahling Katherine, let me in on the secret," said Hilda.

"I said this about old Windy—he is sensible about his service uniform and his desert garb, but he doesn't know shit about a woman," Dr. Katie laughed.

***

The Men's Suitcases

On the other side of the bus, the men had opened their trunk and stared at the contents. Inside, the white traditional *Thoab* overgarments and pants glared in the sunlight. Reynolds grabbed the overgarment and held it away from him to inspect it.

"It looks outstanding on me. Don't you agree? I look like a Bedouin," said Reynolds.

"No," said Windridge, unfolding his garments and looking at them. He eyed Reynolds and commented, "You look like a piece of shit Bedouin—like your brother, the twin turd."

Changing the subject, Windridge called out, "Ladies, while on the trail, you're to help out on the food rations. You two just eat a couple mouthfuls of sand at noon chow. Plus, we'll be saving on water by you two not drinking," Windridge added with a little snicker as he turned away. Hook stared at him wide-eyed.

"I'll go check on the women," Windridge muttered.

He rounded the front of the bus and watched as the women pranced around in their silky black garments. His eyes landed on Dr. Katie and lingered as she smiled and laughed with the others.

***

Meeting the Camels

Old Li approached the bus and announced, "Ladies and gentlemen, please gather around."

His long white ponytail made him appear to be in his mid-seventies, wise in age. He paused as the group assembled in front of the bus.

"I speak enough English to tell you my way or the highway." He introduced the men standing next to him.

"This is my head-puller, Haidar the Short. And this is Sarban, Zian, Bahram, and Yama," said Old Li as they acknowledged each other. "These men will tend to your needs—setting up the yurts, making the campfire with dried camel dung, cooking the food, milking the female camels for wholesome milk, and making cheese," Old Li chuckled.

"One thing you should know: Sarban and Zian have had their tongues cut out by warlords. The other two—they do not say camel shit unless they have a mouthful of it. Ha ha! So all you have to do is enjoy this long, epic ride."

Old Li smiled pleasantly and nodded to each of them before gesturing toward the herd of camels.

"Remember this when riding a camel—go with the sway. Ladies, I am giving you the four most comfortable camels. Each of you will have a *la lo-t'o-ti*, which is to say, 'camel puller.' We have mounted a small *Houdah*, or seat as you say, with oversized *cushy for your tushy*."

He laughed before continuing, "Gentlemen, my men have picked a camel for each of you."

He paused. "Before we get started, most honored ones, I must tell you about the camel you're going to be riding. This camel is called a *Bactrian*—it has two humps. It is a large beast, almost six feet tall and weighing over 1,000 pounds."

He smirked. "It is wise to give your camel a name, like a pet. Take a few minutes to think of one."

Old Li let the group move closer to their camels. The beasts stood still, making their presence known with grunts, bellows, and the occasional loud fart.

Boone circled his camel, inspecting it. "He looks like old Bob Brick, a classmate of mine. Might end up acting just like him too—stubborn."

Doc took the reins of hers and studied its long brown mane. "I'll call mine Betty."

"She looks like sunshine," said Valentina, eyeing the camel's bright blonde humps. "So, *Sunshine* it is."

Windridge eyed the two Marines as they grinned at him.

"I'm going to name mine *Winthorpe*," said Reynolds, smirking.

Hook chimed in, "Well, hell's bells! That's the name I was going to use, you thief! I'll just change mine to *Winthorpe II*."

Windridge's face turned beet red as Reynolds grinned.

Dr. Katie, watching his reaction, smirked. "*Windy*, with an 'I,' not an 'E'."

Windridge clenched his jaw. "You dumb shits…"

CHAPTER 19 - THE FIRST 1000 MILES

Old Li put his hand on Doc's camel and said in broken English, "You enter Silk Road. First thousand miles be uneventful. Once the camel puller tug on your camel's nose, you give swats on camel's ass and that day starts. Eventually, newness wear off after two months. Then, the sun and the sand—and I mean no beach. Tough on female skin." He chuckled.

Each of them mounted their camels, adjusting in the saddle. They waited for the camel pullers to tug on the reins, signaling the start of another long day.

***

"Old Li was right, Katie," said Doc as they rode side by side. "The first 200 miles have been pretty uneventful, but these seven days have been nothing but travel, set up camp, chow, bed, break camp, ride."

"Yes, but we've learned to make a yurt."

The women laughed for a moment before falling into silence. The only sounds were the wind, the bellowing of the camels, the shouts of the camel pullers, and the clang of equipment. Sand coated every inch of the caravan.

Katie broke the silence, "Doc, with the sand and dirt coating us, a little rain will turn us into concrete statues."

The air fell still again, save for the rhythmic sway of the camels beneath them.

The dunes loomed above the caravan, the landscape ever-shifting with the wind. Footprints and shadowy figures from the previous day had vanished, erased as if no one had ever passed. Only the camel pullers knew the way forward. It was a wasteland of endless, rolling dunes where losing one's way was as easy as breathing.

The blazing sun bore down relentlessly. No clouds. No shade. Only when the sun dipped behind the dunes did they find relief from the glare and heat.

Days turned into weeks, with the caravan inching its way westward. Each day, thirty endless miles—grueling, monotonous, and unchanging. Yet, so many more remained.

The nights were filled with routine—setting up camp, cooking food, tending to the camels, and fixing whatever had broken during the day. The simple act of stopping felt like a reward. As darkness blanketed the desert, the temperature plummeted. The warmth of the manure-fed fire was welcome, its acrid smoke less so.

At the end of each night, the group gathered around, exchanging stories. The Marines recounted tales of boot camp, wartime escapades, and barracks brawls. The doctors spoke of medical school, bizarre surgeries, and cases that made even the battle-hardened men squirm.

One such night, Reynolds stood and cleared his throat. "I have a story about Madame Wang's."

Windridge cut him off with a bark. "At ease, Boot. There are ladies present. You're not telling any stories about Wang's."

"Dahling," Dr. von Haag purred, smirking. "I would love to hear such tales about getting tail."

The group chuckled, some shifting to make themselves more comfortable as Reynolds prepared to begin.

He launched into his story, acting out every character, his animated gestures bringing the tale to life. The group erupted in laughter, save for Windridge, who scowled, arms crossed, unimpressed.

When Reynolds finally wrapped up, wiping a tear from his eye, Windridge pushed himself up to his feet. "Reynolds, come with me a minute." Without waiting for a response, he disappeared behind a yurt.

Reynolds hesitated but followed. "Yes, Sergeant, what do you need?"

Without warning, Windridge cocked his arm back and threw a solid punch straight into Reynolds's stomach. The impact sent him doubling over, gasping.

"Have a good night, Squid," Windridge muttered before walking off into the dark.

Back at the fire, the others were beginning to rise, stretching sore muscles and preparing for another night in the desert chill.

Boone dusted off his hands and addressed the group. "Everyone, the guides tell me that tomorrow we reach the eleven-hundred-kilometer mark. That's around eight hundred miles we've traveled on the ships of the desert."

A few groans mixed with nods of acknowledgment. It had felt like more.

Tomorrow would be just another day of sun, sand, and sore asses.

***

"Cold at night. Very mundane. Day in and day out," said Doc, talking through her husband, not at him. "We stopped along the Silk

Road at a place called Wuwei, then Zhangye, then we stopped for the day, and for some reason, Katie pissed off her camel, Windy."

Doc took another drag of her cigarette, flicking her little fingernail with her thumbnail. "Man, oh man, did it pick up after that! We came into a nice shaded area with plenty of water around. Windy—that's the name of Katie's camel, with an I and not an E—went down to his knees. Katie slung her right leg over, and her foot accidentally hit Windy right in the puss!"

Doc chuckled. "Once she got off, the camel puked on her back! She was wearing that beautiful black silk, then it was Katie bar the door!"

"Katie, we can wash it out. Don't worry about it," Doc had assured her.

But Katie responded in old Gaelic, "Gaofar, Tú seafóideach Fásach Bó mhara."

"She laid a right cross into the snout of Windy—with an I and not an E," said Doc.

Then Katie translated in English, "Windy, you feather-brained desert sea cow."

"That was so damn funny! Everything seemed to go in slow motion after that. The camel's snout, full of snot, mouth full of cud spittle and stomach bile, flung to the right, hitting Windridge in the face and chest," Doc recalled.

"Then Windy got up, bellowed hideously, and ran about 20 yards before he could be contained!" she laughed. "After that, Katie and Windy were the best of friends."

She took another long drag before continuing. "Then, around the village of Yumen, we witnessed our first Japanese transports with a bomber escort."

Everyone looked at each other, waiting for the rest of the story. Doc nodded toward the President, General Sullivan, and her new husband.

***

"Lt. Boone," said Reynolds.

"What can I do you for you, Sgt. Reynolds?"

"Sir! Look to the west by southwest. That looks to be about six aircraft. Sir, do you have your binoculars handy?" said Reynolds. Boone found his binoculars and located the aircraft.

"Holy shit, it looks like four Japanese bombers and two transports," said Boone.

"Skipper, what you got?" barked Windridge as he led General Smedley to stand near Boone and look in the same direction.

Then Rev. Black chimed in, "What is the conundrum, brother Boone?"

"There are Japanese transports and bombers flying West by Southwest?" said Boone.

"It looks like they came from Shanghai to Nanjing," said Rev. Black as he looked up to the sky. Rev Black mumbled, "This is falling into place."

"Did you say something, Padre?" said Lt. Boone.

"No, my son, I was starting to pray," Rev. Black said, then he turned to Old Li and instructed, "Old man, let us hasten the camels. I want to stretch the miles out to more than we've been doing."

***

At sunrise, Rev. Black addressed the group, "This morning, we are going to part ways. I'm taking my men and camels when we get to Guazhou, we're going to head toward the city of Dunhuang. My men and I are on a mission from God. We should reach Guazhou at about 3:00 and set up camp outside the city."

"Old Li observed more Jap transports being escorted by fighters, they slowly took a left arc heading south," Rev. Black continued, "Old Li thinks they are headed toward Dunhuang and that area."

"Fighters? Did I hear fighters?" asked Windridge.

Valentina asked, "Where did they get the petrol to fly that distance?"

"Good question," Boone said, taking off his cap and scratching his head.

In the sweltering heat of the afternoon, they found a small oasis. The group decided to set up their yurts for the night.

"I have a detailed map of the routes that we should use," said Old Li as everyone gathered together around a well-worn table as he unfolded the wrinkled and hand-drawn map, pointing to where they would make the split.

"Rev. Black, Haidar the short. You will go on the southern Silk Road route. Myself and the rest of the men, and the women, will go the middle Silk Road," Old Li explained. "My group will be heading west toward Jiuquan where we will stay a couple of days and rest. Next will be Hami. It will take us about six weeks to reach the oasis at Turpan."

Rev. Black explains, "My brothers and I are on a separate mission from God. We will be trying to convert souls to our way of thinking. It was a religious experience to walk with you on this pathway. Godspeed, brothers and sisters."

Each of the group shook his hand and wished him safe travels.

Rev. Black turned his back and walked away with his brothers.

Within moments, Old Li had gathered his herd and his group of travelers and set off on their westward journey.

Each day, the daylight blended into night, and the night into day. The group didn't know, and didn't care, what day of the week it was—they just knew it was another 30 miles, day after day after day.

***

"Hey, limp mode! Why are you limping?" said Windridge.

"Winthorpe bit me right in the ass!" said Reynolds, rubbing his backside.

"Ha, ha, ha! So, why aren't you rubbing your head instead?" said a rather elated Windridge. "How many times does that make now?"

"That's number four," said Reynolds, still rubbing his backside.

"It's working!" gushed Windridge.

"What's working, Gunny?" replied Reynolds, his face wincing.

"I whisper in your camel's ear—and your twin sister camel too when you're not around. I'm telling them to bite, spit, and puke on you two. If they only had thumbs, then they could choke the shit out of you! Or have them fall over on both of you, breaking your legs! Then I could shoot you two like the jackasses you are. The camel actually has some value!" said Windridge with an evil chagrin on his face.

Then Sgt. Hook walked up to Reynolds and Gunny, rubbing the back of his right arm.

Windridge smirked. "Sgt. Head, why are you rubbing the back of your right arm?"

"That piece of shit camel just nipped the back of my arm," said Hook as he showed Windridge and Reynolds.

Windridge came back sarcastically. "A miracle on the Silk Road! One day, men are going to land on the moon. When they get up there and find out that it's really made of smelly turd Limburger cheese—like you two turd buckets."

"Gunny, why would that be a miracle?" said Hook.

"Ha, ha!" Windridge laughed in a caustic tone. "No more than two minutes ago, I was telling Sgt. Brainless right here that I had been whispering to his Winthorpe—and Winthorpe Two! I hoped that camel would whisper to your camel to nip, bite, puke on you, or even choke you out! If they had thumbs. As I told Sgt. Sally Jane Rotten Crotch standing right next to you, I wished your buddy would roll on you, breaking your legs! Then I could put you both down. I'd only need one shot!" He pointed at their heads. "I would put your heads side by side. Then I'd pull the trigger—nothing would impede it! In one ear and out the other."

"By the way, girls, you got the 12 to 4 shift. Any questions? I didn't think so. See you tonight, ladies," said Windridge as he gave the United States Marine Corps Gunnery Sergeant's death look.

"Have you noticed that we do get the 12 to 4 shift a lot?"

"I thought it was a permanent post. Am I wrong? Please tell me I just made $75.60 to get nipped by a camel?" exclaimed Hook as he looked at his buddy, shaking his head, still rubbing the back of his arm.

Reynolds, still rubbing his backside, said, "I'm going to go put my yurt up, get some food, and catch some rack time before 12." Hook agreed.

"What time is it?" whispered Hook.

"You just asked me 10 minutes ago. It's zero dark," whispered Reynolds.

They patrolled the area. Individual yurts dotted the landscape. The bright stars and the desert moon illuminated the surroundings.

Fires, fueled by camel dung, burned lazily in the desert night. Soft desert winds blew lightly, and glowing embers danced away from the fire.

"Chris, did you hear something?" said Hook.

"I did! But I don't know what it was."

"It came from that area! There are some large sand dunes—you could almost hide around them," said Hook.

They crawled on their stomachs to the rise of a dune. Looking down into a small open area, they saw two yurts and two camel dung-fueled fires.

Reynolds whispered to Hook, "Who is down there?"

"Your guess is as good as mine," whispered Hook.

Then, on the far side of the fires, a silhouette of a woman appeared, scantily dressed in black silk. A male figure walked out of a yurt wearing only his boots, a .45 pistol with a belt, and a campaign hat.

"Oh my God, no!" partially bellowed Hook as Reynolds' hand clamped over his mouth.

***

"Gunnery Sgt. Windridge! Why did you stop?" said a seductive, sassy, Irish-toned Dr. Katie Quinncannon.

"I thought I heard some bellowing," said Windridge in his strong voice as he flicked his cigarette toward the camel dung-infused fire, looking to his left in the direction of Reynolds and Hook.

"Just those damn infernal beasts—just doing their normal bellowing," said Dr. Katie. Then, in the form of a beguiling seductress, she added, "Windy, never mind that. (Tú fearga stoda muirí! Bac mé feicim bhur camall teanga?)"

"Ma'am, I have no idea what you just said," insisted Windridge.

Katie smirked. "I said, 'You virile, stud Marine! Let me see your camel tongue.'" She tilted her head, her tone turning commanding. "Now, if you could be so kind as to march your arse over here—now."

"Yes, Mistress Katherine D'Arcy," said Windridge in a submissive tone as the voices faded away into the yurt.

Hook and Reynolds crawled back off the dune. Reynolds turned to Hook, his eyes wide with amusement. In a laughing, entertaining way, he whispered in German:

"*Heute Abend, Winthrop ist ein Mann! Er hat seine Cherry Pie gegessen, mit einer Zuteilung von Schlagsahne! Danach eine Chesterfield in einer Hand, eine Tasse heißen Dr. Katie in der anderen!*"

Then, quickly adding, "You're too slow to process! I'll tell you what I said," laughed Reynolds. "Tonight, Winthrop is a man! He has eaten his cherry pie, with a ration of whipped cream! Afterwards, a Chesterfield in one hand, a cup of hot Dr. Katie in the other!"

Hook shot back in German:

"*Ja, habe ich! Der arme Winthrop wurde von Dr. Katie mit Schlagsahne pussy willow-gepeitscht! Sie ließ ihn ihre Herrin Katherine D'Arcy nennen!*"

Reynolds smirked. "So?"

"Yes!" Hook shot back, then repeated in English, "Yes, I did! Poor Winthrop has been pussy willow whipped by Dr. Katie! She let him call her Mistress Katherine D'Arcy!"

Neither of them could contain their laughter.

Reynolds grinned. "Just like last year. He was in his quarters."

As they both lit a Chesterfield, Hook replied, "That seems so long ago. I wonder what's happening in the world of Madam Wang's?"

Then Hook suddenly stiffened. "Oh, shit, I hope he didn't see us." His face went from pure joy to almost panicky.

Reynolds chuckled. "We should know in about two minutes." He checked his watch. "If he did, he'd be walking over that dune." He smirked. "Remember the cup of hot Joe."

Both Hook and Reynolds laughed again.

Reynolds looked up. "Look at that clear sky! There might be fireworks."

Hook grinned. "Red, white, and blue with a big bang!" They started giggling like two little girls.

After a moment, Hook turned serious. "Chris, let me ask you a serious question."

Reynolds glanced at him. "Shoot."

"When's the last time you saw old Gunny smile? Or be happy?" Hook asked thoughtfully.

Reynolds considered. "That all makes sense now! A couple nights ago," he remarked. "Winthrop tried to nip me, then I dodged a big ol' regurgitated bullet! But what was odd about it—Winthrop seemed to be enjoying it! Gunny saw that, then he just put on the biggest, shittiest grin I've ever seen."

"I don't mean that way," Hook clarified. "I mean the kind of happy that makes a man whole. A home. A good wife. Kids. Family. Extended family. Friends. All in the Marine Corps—or whatever service you picked."

Reynolds laughed. "Well, we have a home—and a mother? Oh boy. Who is also a Gunnery Sergeant. And we're his two kids. But it looks like he's getting his chevrons clipped by dear old dad, Dr. Katie!" He smirked, then added, "Yes, Mistress Katherine D'Arcy." Another round of laughter followed.

Hook grinned. "Don't you mean, 'Ja, Herrin Katherine D'Arcy'?"

Another burst of laughter echoed in the desert night.

"Come to think of it," said Hook, "the last time anything nice happened to Gunny was when we all got our Soochow medals in '32. Then again, just last August—the last 13 years straight of winning the regimental shooting competition! After each one of those shoots, he backed off of us for about two to three days. Then the beast would come back for more carnage."

Hook glanced up. "Oh look, it's our relief! Good morning, sir," he said.

"Morning, Miss Brandt," said Reynolds.

"Good morning, gentlemen," replied Lt. Boone.

"Good morning," Valentina added.

"Anything exciting go on last night, boys?" asked Lt. Boone, sounding as if he'd had a good night's sleep.

"Sir! With all due respect, may we speak to you alone?" said Reynolds.

Boone frowned. "So, how can I help you?"

"Sir, something extraordinary happened to Gunny last night!" said Reynolds.

"What would that be, Sergeant?" Boone replied.

"Sir, it's not what we saw, but what we heard. The sensitivity of that particular material will not be disclosed—because of the nature of the incident while on guard duty. Sir, with all due respect, it's NCO business," explained Hook.

Boone raised an eyebrow. "And?"

Reynolds smirked. "But man to man, there is a maximum probability that Gunny and Dr. Katie played cough and doctor. They played hot coffee and cream! Because Gunny put the grinds in—

fornicating follies, copulating cuties, harbormaster and docking the ship, an artillery round in the breech, a train into a tunnel, mail in the drop box…"

Hook shook his head back and forth. "Sir, Esmeralda felt sorry for Quasimodo! In other words, Dr. Katie and Gunny swapped spit—with bodily fluids through a physical liaison."

"Camel crap!" Boone burst into laughter. "I just lost a bet with Doc! She took yesterday, I took tomorrow night, Valentina had Saturday, Hilda had Tuesday—and Old Li just laughed about it! As they say in America, Doc hit the nail on the head! We all wondered when that volcano was going to blow."

Reynolds grinned. "First one or two times could be from battles and range dirt," he said, looking at his buddies with a big smile.

"A word to the wise, sir—Gunny's elation lasts about two to three days. Plus, one other thing, sir. Sand."

Boone raised an eyebrow. "What about sand?"

"Sir, Gunny's in field mode. He's going to conserve water. Plus, being on cloud nine, sir… You ever been chafed, grated, raw down there because of sand?" Reynolds asked, then turned to Hook. "Hooky, remember old Cpl. Higginbotham? We went to the Philippines for a month of training. He was five hours late for a four-hour pass with those two beautiful indigenous female personnel from the beach. They told him to grab his weapon, then threw on his field pack, and then—on his head, his face—by Gunny Masterson! And to add insult to injury, Gunny Masterson threw an additional 50 pounds on for a 25-mile road march."

Reynolds smirked. "Sir, the sand just tore him up. We're going to be getting on and off camels, then walking for a while. He'll start walking a little funny, sir. You know, like you officers that got a corncob stuck up your ass! Old Gunny's constitution is going to wane. Just a fair warning, sir."

***

"Hey, sunshines, wake up," said a friendly-voiced Windridge.

"Time to get up!" said a sleepy Hook.

"Didn't like your yurt?" asked Windridge.

"Decided to sleep under the open stars, keeping warm near a shitty fire. I told Reynolds last night to throw his leg in the fire," said Hook as he rubbed the sleep from his eye.

"I even brought you boys coffee and chow," said Windridge, handing them each a cup. "It's an outstanding day to be a Marine! In about two more months, it'll be the Marines' 163rd birthday—and finally, we'll get this mission over with!" A rather happy Gunny grinned. "And just because I'm in a good mood, I'll give you boys a couple of weeks off from the 12-to-4 watch. Dr. Katie and I will take that shift."

As he crouched down, he lit both of their cigarettes.

"Good morning, sir! Morning, Valentina," said a pleasant Windridge. Then, turning back, he asked, "So, what's the plan, Skipper?"

"We're to break camp and start making tracks as soon as possible. I just talked to Old Li," Boone conveyed. "Our next destination is Karashar—the Iron Gate. We'll pass through that to get to Korla."

"Gentlemen," Valentina addressed the group. "If you were to refurbish a lady of the evening, where would you send her for one year of treatment?"

They all shrugged as if to say, *I don't know.*

"The Virgin Islands," Valentina answered before walking away, leaving them all standing in silence.

"Day one, done," said Reynolds as he and Hook walked their camels.

A little ways away, Hilde turned to her companion. "Darling, I've been meaning to ask—how are you holding up with Betty and Sue? I know you don't say much about it since that unfortunate day months ago. You know, sweetie, I'm a surprisingly good listener too," she said in her German accent as they walked their camels.

"Now, boys, that we're all settled in for the night, we can have a little nightcap," said Windridge.

Both Hook and Reynolds looked on in amazement as Gunny produced a three-quarters full bottle of Bushmills.

"Gunny, where did you get that?" asked Reynolds.

"Acquisitions and procurement from the Godly Rev. Black's gear—just before we split west and he went south," said Windridge.

They took a shot of Bushmills straight from the bottle, then lit their Chesterfields, reminiscing about the old days while staring into a camel dung-infused fire for a half-hour before drifting off to sleep.

"Hooky," said Reynolds, "two full days have gone by, and we've yet to draw fire."

"No shit, Sherlock! But when that dam breaks, you don't want to be around those rounds," said Hook, relief on his face. Then he added, "We're coming up on Korla. I hope Dr. Katie keeps helping."

"Gunny! Look—home sweet home for the night!" said Reynolds.

Gunny scoffed. "Limp mode, what's so fucking sweet about it? Does that sand look like grains of sugar to you, numb nuts? My ass, my nuts—are so fucking chafed down there from the sand! Getting on and off with General Smedley, then walking that bastard. And just like Navy chow, it tried to puke on me!"

Then, bellowing, "When's the last time you boys did your two echelons of camel maintenance?! Remember—echelon one, stick your head up their ass! Echelon two, get the compacted sand out—lickety-split!" Windridge gave them a cruel and unusual grin.

"Top of the morning, Sgt. Reynolds. Sgt. Hook," said a bright and cheery Dr. Katie as she walked up to the boys.

"Sgt. Windridge, would you care to join me? I could use some protection while I wash up," she asked pleasantly.

"Yes, ma'am, I'll escort you with pleasure!" said Windridge.

As they walked away, Hook turned to Reynolds and whispered, "Winthrop is pussy willow whipped something fierce."

Walking side by side, Dr. Katie turned to Windridge. "I thought I heard you say 'mode'?"

"Yes! I called Reynolds a limp mode!" stated Windridge, rather pleasantly.

Dr. Katie chuckled. "Winthrop, sometimes you're *ceannramhar*."

Windridge furrowed his brow. "What the hell does that mean?"

"In the old tongue? It means *thick head*. It's *lymph node,* not limp mode," she corrected in her Irish tone, grabbing his arm as they continued walking—both bowlegged like they'd just competed in the Cheyenne Frontier Days rodeo.

CHAPTER 20 - HOT JOE AND A 45

"We stayed there about a week," said Doc as Curly lit her cigarette for her.

"Sweetheart, do you need to take a break?" asked Curly.

"No, darling, I'm right as rain," replied Doc. Then, after exhaling her smoke, she continued.

"Finally, Rev. Black's caravan met us at Korla. Unfortunately, Rev. Black came in mortally wounded—he died from gunshot wounds. The Short was also killed," said Doc as she flicked her right thumb and pinky nails.

"About two days after we left Korla, heading south toward Aksu, we ran across a downed Mits3 Japanese bomber," Doc continued, her voice distant as she seemed to be reliving the memory.

"It was full of spare parts—three rail axles, two tank tracks. The pilots and crew were nowhere to be found," she said, looking at the President, Secretary of War, top military brass, OSS, and, of course, her husband. Their faces were a mix of shock, disbelief, and barely contained anger.

General Sullivan slugged down a shot of Bushmills but remained silent, letting her tell her story.

"Gentlemen, I'll explain it like a dinner course."

"First course: Russian generals, commissar officers, NCOs, and enlisted Russians coming from the Central Asian Military District in Tashkent."

"Second course: Deserters from the '36 to '38 Russian purge, hired Cossacks, Afghan mercenaries, and bandits coming over the Tian Shan mountain range from Kazakhstan through Kyrgyzstan."

"Third course: Chinese warlords."

"Dessert course? The Japanese. From that day to the day I left," said Doc.

"We were outside of Kucha, near the ancient temple of Subashi, when one arsehole, as Katie would call them, showed up—this particular Russian, political commissar Vasily Travkin," said Doc.

"Say, Gunny, the hair on the back of my neck has been standing up and tingling for about a day and a half," said Hook.

"That's lice on your asshole, scrotum-head. I suspect you and dribble dick are getting those from camel maintenance," shot back Windridge.

"No! I'm Dick. He just dribbles! Gunnery Sergeant, it's like we're being followed," responded Hook.

"I figured more like two days," said Windridge.

"There are about 60 Cossacks on horseback—pretty well-armed with their rifles, PPD 34/38 submachine guns (their 'burp guns'), and of course, their shashka swords," Windridge added.

Reynolds blinked. "How do you know that, Gunny?"

Then, realization dawned. "Wait a damn minute—holy crap, I just answered my own question."

He turned to Windridge. "You snuck out one night, went back, and took a peek, didn't you, Gunnery Sergeant?"

Windridge smirked. "Shit-for-brains, you're a goddamn brain surgeon! You have the makings of an outstanding moron officer."

Reynolds shot back quickly. "Gunny, bite your tongue. I don't want to be an officer!"

As they walked their camels, Windridge called out, "Boys! Break open the equipment! I'm informing Lt. Boone."

"What do you mean we've been trailed?" Boone asked.

"Yes, sir, going on about two days. They're about a mile out, holding back—which means we might get pinched, with somebody waiting up ahead," said Windridge.

Boone cut him off. "You're thinking we make a stand here? We have good cover. Get everybody together."

Boone looked at his map. "Old Li, have you run into this before?"

"Yes! Numerous times," Old Li responded.

Boone exhaled sharply. "And the end result?"

Old Li shrugged. "I always had to fight. Son of a bitch—sounds like I might lose a few camels today." He walked off toward his men.

Boone nodded. "Old Li, take your camels and get them moving up into the washout. Block the rear and cover the left flank. We'll cover the mouth of the washout."

Turning to Windridge, he ordered, "Gunnery Sergeant, have the boys get our special camels with our weapons."

Windridge smirked. "Sir, NCOs are always one step ahead of an officer."

Boone ignored the jab. "Reynolds, where do you want to set up?"

"We own the high ground! Go to the left, get a good overview of the center, and try to stay out of sight. I'll let you know when to fire. And take Doc with you as lookout," Boone added.

He turned to Windridge. "Gunny, take Dr. Katie to cover the right flank. Old Li and his boys have the left flank and rear. Valentina, Hilda, and I will fill in where needed."

Reynolds sighed. "I'm so excited, I have to tinkle."

Doc, listening, chuckled. "I'll play lookout."

They found an outstanding setup for their machine gun.

"Oh boys, to the left! Coming down from the mountain—I'm seeing dust getting kicked up," said Doc.

Hook squinted. "I don't see a thing." He quickly added, "Not doubting your word, ma'am—you have a set of spotter peepers."

Reynolds agreed. "Nor do I, ma'am. I don't see them."

"Gentlemen, to the left, they're about three-quarters of a mile out," said Doc.

Reynolds nodded. "Ma'am, you have sniper eyes. And I mean that in a constructive way."

"I get what you mean, Sergeant," said Doc.

Then she put her fingers to her lips and let out a surprisingly sharp, shrill whistle.

Lt. Boone, hearing it, looked up.

"About 15 more minutes! The Christmas carolers will be here," Doc yelled down to Boone, who responded with a thumbs-up.

Doc turned back. "What kind of big gun is that?"

"This is a 1917 water-cooled Browning machine gun," said Hook.

Doc frowned. "But it's 1938?"

Reynolds smirked. "No, ma'am, that's the year it came out."

As they assembled and loaded the machine gun, Reynolds grinned. "We call her 'The Old Bitch' because…"

"It's a bitch to haul!"

"It's a bitch to set up!"

"It's a bitch to take apart!"

"She's a real bitch when she gets jammed!"

"She's a bitch to clean!"

"And if you trip with it, the bitch will smash you—especially when she's scalding hot!"

Doc nodded.

Reynolds handed her his .45. "Here, Doc! Take my .45. A round's in the chamber—point and pull the trigger. To reload, push the small button—the clip drops out—then push a new clip in and charge the weapon."

He pointed to the release. "Remember, Doc, you only have seven shots—make 'em count. Here are 10 mags."

Doc studied the pistol. "Where did you learn to whistle like that?" Hook asked.

Doc smirked. "Well, I just pucker and blow."

***

CHAPTER 21 - FIRE!

"No, ma'am, this is called a Thompson .45 caliber machine gun," said Windridge as he explained to Dr. Katie. "Pull that little stubby knob on top all the way back—the bolt is to the rear. This is a 20-round magazine; it slides in sideways. Charge the weapon by letting the bolt go forward—that will chamber a round. We're going to put this on semi-automatic. When you're ready, pull this up to your shoulder, bend forward, aim, then squeeze the trigger and fire away—one at a time!"

Windridge eyed her carefully. "This gun has a lot of kick, and I don't want to see you mopping the air, so hold on to that hand grip—but good!"

He pointed to the release mechanism. "There's a release on this side to drop the magazine. Put this magazine in, let the bolt go forward, and give them hell!"

"They call this thing the 'Chicago Typewriter,'" said Windridge.

Dr. Katie suddenly wrapped her arms around Windridge's neck, planting a firm lip lock on him. Pulling back, she smirked. "Windy, with an I, not an E—I expect you to kick arse and inquire a few names," she said in her Irish brogue before walking away to her position near Windridge.

***

"Dr. von Haag, Valentina, are you ladies ready for this?" Boone asked.

Both nodded.

"Boys, there they are!" said Doc as the Cossacks formed up in front of the washout, about 200 meters from Boone's position.

"One rider is coming this way," said Valentina to Boone and Hilda.

"They're probably coming to parlay. One way or another, we'll find out," Boone said.

"Я хочу поговорить с тем, кто здесь главный! A Rev. Black. I am Colonel Василий Travkin, сотрудник по политическим вопросам в этом регионе!" the Russian officer called out.

Boone frowned. "Damn it, I don't speak Russian! What about you, Valentina?"

"It's rusty at best," she admitted.

"I speak perfect Russian, darling," Hilda chimed in.

She listened carefully, then turned to Boone. "He just said, 'I want to speak to the one in charge! A Rev. Black. I am Colonel Vasily Travkin, political officer of this region!'"

Hilda exhaled. "Darling, that would be you, Lieutenant Boone."

Boone sighed. "Darling, I'll need you to translate."

Lighting a cigarette, Boone asked, "Tell him this—why do you need to see Rev. Black?"

Hilda translated into Russian, "Почему вам нужно увидеть преподобного Блэка?"

The Russian colonel responded, "Я приехал с твоим ежемесячным посылом для Безумного Энтони! И скажи преподобному Блэку, что у меня есть его деньги на пулеметы и боеприпасы!"

Hilda translated. "Boone, darling, he said, 'I have come with your monthly shipment for Mad Anthony! And tell Rev. Black I have his money for the machine guns and ammunition!'"

Boone looked at Valentina and Hilda. "Who the hell is Mad Anthony? And what money?"

Both shook their heads.

Boone exhaled sharply. "Hilda, tell that Russian idiot that Rev. Black is dead, and we have no idea what shipment he's talking about."

Hilda smirked as she translated, "Мой друг говорит, что ты большевистский тупица! Преподобный Блэк мертв, ты идиот! Ты должен засунуть свою голову себе в задницу! Плюс, у нас нет понятия о предполагаемой отправке или товаре, о котором ты говоришь, придурок!"

Boone turned his head, barely containing his laughter. The Russian colonel suddenly let out a booming laugh of his own before responding, "Это его беда! Одно товарищество распадается, и образуются новые. Это жизнь, которую мы ведем! Но несмотря ни на что, я должен доставить груз Безумному Энтони другим способом. В любом случае, у вас есть одна минута, а затем мы вас всех убьём и заберём ваших верблюдов! Позвольте мне исправиться: мы убьём вас, ваших людей, а затем возьмём верблюдов, женщин и ваши деньги, Дьявол-Пёс!"

Boone raised an eyebrow. "Hilda, what did squid have to say?"

Hilda translated. "That is his misfortune! One partnership dissolves, and new ones form. That is the life we lead. But no matter what, he must get the shipment to Mad Anthony by other dubious means. In any case, we have one minute before he plans to kill us all and take our camels. Correction—he said he will kill you and your men, then take the machine guns, ammunition, camels, women, and your money, Devil Dog."

Boone chuckled. "Cocky little bastard. Ladies, I still don't have a clue what's going on or who the hell Mad Anthony is."

Then he turned and yelled to the group. "As soon as I fire, you may commence fire!"

***

"Oh, I'm so excited! Now I have to take a Hook and wipe my Tomass," said Reynolds, patting his buddy's back.

Hook shot back, singing, "Miss Chris, you squat to piss!"

Now that Colonel Travkin had returned to his men, he pulled his saber. The Cossacks began a slow trot toward the washout in full regalia—an old-school cavalry charge.

Colonel Travkin shouted, "Бесплатно!"

Hilda's eyes widened. "Boone, darling! He yelled 'Charge!'"

"Here they come!" Boone shouted. "Fire!"

Hook and Reynolds opened up with the old Bitch. Boone ramped up his fire. On the right side, Windridge and Dr. Katie unleashed hell with their Thompsons, catching the Cossacks off guard. Bullets tore through the first row, knocking down horses and riders. The second row jumped over their fallen comrades. Colonel Travkin's headless body remained upright, still clutching his reins as his wounded steed pawed at the ground.

"Reload!" shouted Hook.

Reynolds slammed in another 250-round cloth belt.

"Reload!" yelled Windridge.

Dr. Katie shouted something back.

Windridge's eyes narrowed. "Woman, what did you just yell?"

Dr. Katie grinned. "*Sibh aineolach, rúiseach cosac! Tugaim timpeall, bhur claíomh rince chun a meaisínghunna saranáid!*"

Windridge blinked. "The hell does that mean?"

Dr. Katie smirked. "Ye ignorant Russian Cossack! Bring about your sword dance to a machine gun serenade!"

She stood up and emptied half a drum into the retreating cavalry. Windridge followed suit, typing away in the "Chicago typing pool." Hook and Reynolds fed the old Bitch another taste.

Boone raised his hand. "Cease fire!"

Steam rose from the water-cooled Browning. Smoke curled from the Thompsons.

***

"Old Li, how did you make out?" Boone asked.

Old Li's face was grim. "Half a dozen wounded. Four killed. The other two got away with about half a dozen camels. We lost about a dozen more." He spat on the ground. "Our Cossack friends will take a moment to reevaluate their situation."

Boone nodded. "Hook, Reynolds—you two cover the right flank."

They gave a thumbs-up.

"Gunny, Dr. Katie—I need you both down here. We're running low on ammo."

Windridge checked. "Sir, we're short on .30 cal and .45 Thompson rounds."

Boone sighed, "Shotguns and 45 pistols ready?"

Windridge grinned, "Roger that, sir."

Boone turned to Old Li, "How far to our next stop?"

"About 260 km to Aksu."

Boone exhaled. "Let's get moving."

"Roger that, sir! Ladies, this is a shotgun," explained Windridge.

"Lt. Boone, sir, it looks like they're heading north!" Hook called out, spotting dust and riders in the distance.

"Sir, we caught them flat-footed. They didn't expect the old Bitch and Thompsons to chew them a new asshole, sir!" said Windridge.

Boone nodded. "Sgt. Windridge, take your shotgun! You and I are walking out there to check for survivors and any maps or paperwork so Hilda can translate. Doc, be ready in case there are wounded."

Valentina, Hilda, Boone, and Doc cautiously moved through the battlefield, scanning for any sign of life. Then Doc heard a faint moan.

"Lt. Boone, over here!" she called, kneeling beside a wounded Cossack.

Boone knelt down next to her as Doc examined the wound.

"This is a mortal wound to his stomach. All I can do is make him comfortable," said Doc grimly.

Boone was about to respond when Windridge suddenly shouted, "Look out!"

Two Cossacks who had been playing possum sprang up, swords raised, ready to hack down Boone and Doc.

Windridge fired his shotgun—the first round hit one Cossack square in the chest, blowing him back three feet. Without hesitation, he chambered another round and blocked a Cossacks sword blow with his shotgun.

In an instant, Doc raised her pistol and fired. The shot snapped the top of the Cossack's head clean off.

Windridge exhaled. "Lt. Boone, you all right?"

Boone gave a smirk. "Semper Fi."

Doc put down her pistol and checked the wounded Cossack again. "He's gone," she said softly, brushing her right hand over his open eyes to close them.

Boone stood. "We're done here."

Windridge came over, holding a small pile of loot. "Sir, we found three things on the headless Cossack—$100,000 stuffed into two money belts, plus 100 pounds of opium in his saddlebags, sir."

Boone turned to Old Li. "Old Li, you and your men ready to go?"

"Yes," Old Li confirmed.

Boone took a deep breath. "Old Li, how far is our next stop?"

"About 260 km to the next oasis—Aksu," replied Old Li.

Boone nodded. "Then let's move out."

CHAPTER 22 - WHAT'S ON THE FILM?

"We spent about three days at that oasis. Then we pushed on to Kashgar, where we met Davar—Rev. Black's contact," said Doc.

She continued, "He took us to a safe house outside the city. That's where we parted ways with Old Li. He was just a sweetheart—I'm going to miss that old fart," she added, setting her drink down.

"From that point on, Davar told us what we were up against. We traveled by various means, moving at night along the railroad tracks, dodging armored cars, armored trains, and foot patrols, then sleeping during the day," Doc explained.

She took a breath, then continued, "The Japanese built a railhead from Kashgar southeast to their new one at Hotan. That's where their supplies are flown in from one of three routes—north from Peking, center from Xi'an, and south from Shanghai and Nanjing."

Doc looked directly at her husband, who listened without interruption.

"Their first stop by rail was Shule. The second stop was at Yengisar. The third was Yarkant, and now they've stopped at Hotan," she said.

She pulled out some documents and placed them on the table. "Hotan is where they set up the Army, Navy, and special naval Marines' jumping-off point, complete with airfields. I have maps, aerial photographs, and about 20 minutes of aerial footage of these locations, near or on the bases."

The President, Secretary of War, and Mr. Donovan immediately leaned in to examine them.

Doc stood up. "Gentlemen, I've got to go number one."

General Sullivan smirked. "I have to go number two," he said, holding up two fingers and laughing.

Curly chuckled. "I'm tagging along, too."

As they stepped into the hallway, General Sullivan's tone shifted. "Now that we're outside, I need to talk to you two. When you're done with your business, meet me right back here."

A few minutes later, he folded his arms. "Now that our hands are nice and clean…"

He turned to them, his expression serious. "Son. Daughter-in-law. The Army has their meetings, and I have mine. I need you two to come clean with me—about the Silk Road."

Curly frowned. "Sure, Pops. What do you need?"

Sullivan shook his head. "Not you, boy—your wife."

Doc met his gaze. "What would you like to know, sir?"

"You talked to Rev. Black. Did he ever mention the last name of 'Mad Anthony'?"

"No, sir," Doc answered.

Curly frowned. "Dad, what are you driving at?"

Sullivan exhaled sharply. "What I'm driving at, son, is I've gotten early reports—including yours—that lead me to believe Mad Anthony is your mother's brother, Anthony Waugh. Or, as they call him, 'Mad Anthony Waugh.'"

Curly's face darkened as his father continued. "His drug of choice for global distribution is Chinese opium—along with various underworld enterprises: sex slaves, women, children… in some cases, even old people. Some for work, some for pleasure. Then there's his arms dealing. I'm afraid he'll sell to the other side. He's expanding—all in the wrong ways. And now, it looks like he's going to quietly profit from this war."

Doc inhaled deeply. "Well, let me come clean, then."

Both Sullivan and Curly turned their full attention to her.

"I mentioned that downed Japanese bomber—the one with spare parts and equipment?" She paused. "It also had 100 pounds of Chinese opium."

The two men exchanged a look.

Just then, General Sullivan straightened his uniform. "Excuse me, Mr. President, for the delay. Had some family matters to attend to."

The President nodded. "Doc, please continue your story."

Doc settled back into her seat. "By late '38, Davar introduced us to some of the elders and villagers along the Karakax River. They'd saved our lives numerous times—not so much by fighting, but by sharing food, passing messages, and gathering intelligence on the Japs. They helped us survive until we could get back to the Dam."

The Secretary of War interrupted. "How did you get the aerial photographs and footage?"

Doc smirked. "The village elders introduced us to an exotic import-export dealer—a company for select clientele. They help... move merchandise or persons of interest via air."

She examined her nails casually. "And by that, I mean they fly in, export you out, put a parachute on your ass, and drop you wherever you need to go. Within about 200 miles, give or take."

Lighting a cigarette, she added, "With all the damn Jap airplanes running around spitting lead, Wild Bill and what he calls his 'Bats' have to be fast—get in and get out."

She took a drag, then continued. "Never really spoke much to the owner. I did more talking with his daughters—Rachel, the older one, and Clemence. Both of flying age. Their sons went back to France in 1940 to fight for their country."

She leaned back. "Wild Bill's crew—his 'Bats'—were making their way back to the U.S. to see if they could rejoin the Army Air Corps."

She exhaled a slow stream of smoke. "Wild Bill and his wife weren't big talkers. Funny thing, though—on the way out of the plane, his wife looked at me and said, *Au revoir, asshole. Au revoir.*"

She demonstrated the wave the woman had given her.

Curly, shaking his head, let out a low chuckle.

Doc's eyes sparkled mischievously. "She didn't shake my hand. She just waved."

General Sullivan narrowed his eyes, intrigued. "My new daughter-in-law, I'd like to ask you one question."

Doc smirked. "Go ahead and shoot."

"What type of airplane were they using?" he asked, his curiosity obvious.

Doc took a second to think. "Some old World War I planes—Sopwith 1 ½ somethings." She shrugged. "They had a unique squadron symbol—yellow circle with a black bat. The bat's body was shaped like a hand with the center finger extended up. The other four fingers curved down, forming the bat's wings."

She tilted her head. "Why do you ask, sir?"

"It's not important," replied General Sullivan, silently chuckling to himself, a big smile spreading across his face.

Doc took a deep breath. "About four weeks ago, the whole gang and I ran into Major Mo—long enough to kill him. Gentlemen, that is all I'm going to say about that."

Tears welled up in her eyes.

"Sweetheart, you need to take a break," her husband said softly.

"No, no, I don't!" Doc snapped.

She squared her shoulders. "I don't need a break—how about another belt? I have more information to put out." Her voice had a sharper edge.

Curly raised his hands. "Go ahead, doll face! I'm not stopping you."

She slugged back her Bushmills, wiping her mouth with the back of her hand, slightly smudging her lipstick.

The Secretary of War shook his head. "Young lady, this sounds preposterous! You expect us to believe all this buildup by the Japanese Imperial Forces? Then you say you saw fighters and tank parts? Sounds like poppycock."

General Sullivan's aide stepped forward. "Beggin' your pardon, Mr. Secretary, but my men have set up the screen and projector."

The room darkened as the film rolled.

Doc's voice was steady. "Gentlemen, as you can see, the train is heading west to east at that time."

She pointed. "Look at the tops of those railcars—three TK Type 94 tankettes, each with a 6.5 mm machine gun as their main armament. Compare that to the Te-Ke Type 97 tankettes, which are armed with a 37 mm tank gun and a 7.7 mm machine gun. Both have a crew of two. Next railcar—three Type Ha-Go light tanks, also equipped with a 37 mm tank gun and two 7.7 mm machine guns."

She let the images speak for themselves before continuing.

"Now, note the next railcar. There are two types of medium tanks. The Chi-Ha is armed with a 57 mm tank gun and two 7.7 mm machine guns. Then there's the ShinHo, armed with a 47 mm tank gun and also carrying two 7.7 mm machine guns. What you're seeing is a mix of tank regiments from four different divisions."

She paused and pointed again. "See that armored car at the rear of the train? And up front, just ahead of the engine—that's what they call a Sumida armored car. It's armed with a 7.7 mm machine gun and can run on both roads and rails. You'll notice they're coupling them in pairs."

Doc exhaled, her voice darkening. "You'll also notice two rail lines. The narrow gauge is for transporting troops and equipment under guard. The standard gauge is for hauling normal-sized loads. The heavy loads are airlifted in, piece by piece, then assembled in blacksmith shops in Kashgar and now Hotan."

She let that sink in before continuing. "As you've seen, they've moved in tanks, artillery, armored personnel carriers, and troops. And then there are the radar stations."

The Secretary of War leaned forward. "Radar stations?"

Doc nodded. "Yes, and they serve a dual purpose. They also act as beacons for the three fuel routes into Western China. Plus, gentlemen—all of this track was laid by dead slave labor and those still breathing."

The film continued rolling.

"The next five minutes cover their air capabilities," Doc said.

The footage showed a series of revetments—fortified bunkers protecting aircraft.

"They have two air groups—half fighters, half reconnaissance and bomber escorts. Then there's the heavy bomber air group, made up of Mits G3s and Mits G4s, along with various heavy transport aircraft. These planes come from multiple air groups—about 120 fully operational aircraft, moving in and out of Kashgar. Now that Hotan is operational, they have even more."

The room was silent.

"The airfields were also built by slave labor," she added.

The film ended.

Doc's voice remained steady. "That doesn't even count the two regiments of artillery. Or the nearly 60,000 infantry split between heavy and light divisions. They even have Japanese Army paratroopers. And then, of course, there are 25,000 Special Naval Landing Forces—their so-called Marines."

She paused before delivering the final blow. "The entire operation is being run by the Central China Expeditionary Army out of Peking. Furthermore, their main Army and Naval air base is in Chungking, Szechuan Province. When you add them up—ballpark estimate? 125,000 men between Kashgar and Hotan. That's just over 600 miles from Delhi."

General Sullivan leaned toward his son. "Son," he whispered, "I don't think your wife—my new daughter-in-law—realizes she's rambling… but educational rambling."

Curly nodded, still processing the magnitude of what he had just heard.

The Secretary of War suddenly spoke up. "Oh, I thought the pilot was female—because there's a sergeant sitting there now in his Marine uniform, smiling."

The film abruptly cut to black.

The Secretary of War turned sharply. "What else is on that film?"

The room tensed.

"And who's that sergeant?" he demanded.

Doc didn't flinch. "Sir, his name is Sgt. Reynolds. And that, sir, is NCO business."

The lights came back on.

Colonel Donovan cleared his throat. "Doc... may I call you Doc?"

She nodded. "By all means."

"Tell us more about the Dam," he asked.

Doc leaned back. "I would've called it the Batcave, but that name's taken."

She smirked before continuing. "Funny thing you mention it—Rachel told me her father had finally set it up the way he wanted, then left for the United States, putting Rachel and Clemence in charge."

She gestured toward the map. "Inside the mountain, there's a 1,000-foot runway, wide enough to accommodate large planes. It's an optical illusion with speed—on top of the dam, they grow cotton. The Karakax River winds hard from Hotan. From there, they radio ahead that you're heading south. When you reach the cotton field, you take a sharp right—right into the face of the mountain. They pull the wall back, and once you're in, they close it. Any dumb-ass Nips chasing you? They keep following the river. The inside of that mountain is carved out into a small city—hospital with 12 beds, mess hall, barracks, workshops."

She flicked her cigarette. "We also run operations out of there, traveling by river at night into Hotan."

Her voice sharpened. "This is their jumping-off point. Pardon me, Mr. President, but they'll bomb the shit out of Delhi—and they could reach Bombay. We figure they're coming through the back door, drawing British forces away from Burma, exactly where they're needed."

Colonel Donovan's tone was grave. "Dr. Sullivan, I'm about to tell you something that only a handful of people know—and most of them are in this room."

He continued. "Great Britain requested we run a PIC operation. PIC stands for Passive Information Collection—photos, maps, funding, weapons. We sent a team of six agents to China. Only one returned."

Doc's expression tightened.

Colonel Donovan's voice was low. "That one? That was your husband."

Silence.

"Brother Green," he continued. "Rev. Black was in charge. Brothers Silver, Gray, Black, and Red are all confirmed dead—according to your reports."

He exhaled, running a hand through his hair. "And now, with this new information… the scope is far larger than we thought."

"So, Capt. Sullivan, how come I didn't see you on the trail?" Doc asked, scrutinizing him.

Curly smirked. "Simple fact is, I spent six months in a local hospital just outside Niya."

He sighed and leaned back. "A local kid was kicking a ball around, and it went over some flimsy fence. I stopped to grab a bite to eat, gave the kid a couple of bucks to take care of the horse, and told him I'd fetch his ball. Bent down, head toward the fence—BAM! A drunk driver crashed through it, hit me square on top of the head."

He grinned. "Flipped me right over the top of the car! Broke my leg, collarbone, arm, and a couple of ribs. But the real lollapalooza?"

He bent down. "I want you to look at these four grill marks indented in my head."

Everyone leaned in, gawking.

Doc shook her head and turned to Colonel Donovan. "Who was Rev. Black?"

Colonel Donovan exhaled. "His name was Dan Black. Captain, Navy Intelligence. I thought he was one of our top men." He scratched his head. "But I don't understand the opium."

Doc nodded. "The only thing the Russian said to me was, 'If I don't deliver this, I'm a dead man.' And then he died."

Colonel Donovan leaned forward. "So, what happened to the opium?"

"We took it to the hospital and used it to help the villagers," Doc said. "The Japanese have been beating or killing them since 1938. Until about three weeks ago, there were ten of us fighting and killing Japs. Been lucky—real lucky. Close enough that drops of their sweat have fallen on me." She knocked hard on the wooden desk.

"So far, we've convinced the Japs we're just bandits. We dress and act the part—ambush and rob."

General Sullivan took a long breath, his Irish brogue thickening. "Young lady, I barely know you, but I feel like I've known you all my life. That's why I have a large favor to ask. I'm not asking as your father-in-law—I'm asking as the General of the Army. I would understand if you said no after what you've been through... but your country needs you. I need you. We're on the cusp of another world war—one far worse than the last carnage."

Doc didn't hesitate. "What does my country need me to do, sir?"

The General paused, choosing his words carefully.

"I need you to—" He exhaled. "We need you to go back to China. Do the same thing you've been doing—harassment, cutting supply and communication lines, guerrilla warfare. But this time, take your husband with you. He's the only reinforcement I can give you right now."

He rubbed the back of his head. "Recruit warlords, deserters, mercenaries—anyone who can fight. We'll pay them."

Doc crossed her arms. "General, I got a real smart lady back in China who can handle that diplomacy—with some bite. Her name's Valentina."

She tilted her head. "When do we ship out?"

Curly chuckled. "Sweetheart, we don't ship out. In the Army, we move out at a high rate of speed."

Doc smirked. "Oh, I see. When do we move out at a high rate of speed, Capt. Sullivan?"

General Sullivan grinned. "That's Major Sullivan now. And since you're a medical doctor, you automatically receive a commission. Effective as of today's date, you are Major F.F. Sullivan."

He leaned in. "But you won't fall under the Medical Corps. You'll fall under the new OSS along with my darling son and that ragtag bunch."

Curly raised an eyebrow. "And who's the officer in charge out there?"

Doc answered without hesitation. "Lt. Boone."

Sullivan nodded. "Tell him he's Capt. Boone now—once Major Sullivan gets established out there."

He turned to his aides. "Tell the other doctors they're commissioned as Captains."

He looked back at Doc, a rare softness in his eyes. "You'll be getting more help and equipment soon. I can promise you that, little lady. You're my new daughter-in-law—Mary Magdalene would kill me if I let anything happen to you."

He shot Curly a glance. "Sorry, son, but you're in the backwater of the backwater now."

Curly grinned. "Wouldn't have it any other way, sir."

The General studied Doc. "Doc, are you related to Frank and Harold Kendall?"

Doc blinked. "Yes! They're my older brothers. I have one older sister, Claire Ann, and one younger sister, Wilhelmina. Why do you ask?"

Sullivan's expression darkened. "Because you just missed them."

Doc's heart pounded. "What?"

"Frank went to a little place called Wake Island, smack dab in the middle of the Pacific. Harold? He went to the Philippines— handcuffed to a briefcase—headed to see Doug MacArthur."

The room fell silent.

The General straightened his uniform. "I think we're done here."

One by one, they shook hands, exchanging well wishes.

The Sullivans were going to war. Again.

CHAPTER 23 - PAY THE PIPER

"Sgt. Bonnie to the Munitions buildings ASAP!" Said General Sullivan.

"Yes sir," replied Sgt. Bonnie.

"Son, I would like to introduce you to Mrs. Crumley! my personal secretary Agnes! this is my new daughter-in-law! just call her Doc," said the General as they all shook hands.

"General your staff is assembled in the office! and may I say sir! that is quite a unique collection of men?" said Mrs. Crumley. as laughter to bull shitting to harder laughter could be heard on the other side of that door. as the door to General Sullivan's office was open, there sat a conglomeration of men, with happy war weary faces! glad to see their old commander and friend! only grayer and longer in the tooth.

"Oh my, look the cat drug in!" said Sgt. Major. Wilson.

"I thought I was quietly! going to retire! right into private practice instead you! give me another star and told me, to come here!" said Lt. General James O'Keefe known as Doc.

"Boys, we have a humdinger rolling up on us pretty quick!" said General Sullivan.

"Doc, I need you take care of the physical side of the medical," said Sullivan.

"Roger that Gen!"

"Mr. Forthright, I see that you squared away the First Infantry Division like I asked," said General Sullivan.

"Only a little ass kicking here and there."

"Sgt. Majors John and Tom Lightfoot, I see you two took care the 25th Infantry Division in Hawaii!" stated Sullivan.

"I really appreciate it Crow! I mean Gen," said Thug.

"When I wasn't in the Army! I was laying on the beach watching hula girls, with an umbrella drink in the fetal position! Ready to be ripped away from this one day! and since you ripped me and the old man away! It must be some doozy!" said Tom Lightfoot.

"I wasn't in the fetal! I personally was stretched out watching hula girls with my umbrella drink! enjoying the sun! huh like I! need more sun! and the surf, with sand in my crotch," said John Lightfoot.

"Well, pumpkin patches and poison ivy, I wonder when y'all gonna call me back?" said Lt. General Decatur Shea. In his distinct Georgia accent.

"When did you get back into town! old man?" said Sullivan. as he shook and hugged all his buddies.

"Just about an hour ago, long enough to find drink or two! those three years in Germany? that old boy over there, terrible case of alligator mouth! but with a bite," said Shea. then there's a knock at the door and in walks Colonel Ronald Smedley.

"Smedley old man! somebody made you a Colonel?" said Wilson. As he scratched his head.

"I did, you walking buffoon!" shot back Sullivan.

"I wonder that myself?" replied Smedley.

"I thought, you're the Dean of English at the University of Nebraska, what happened?" said Wilson.

"General Sullivan called and said he needed me to help run communications; so here I am!" said Smedley.

"General Sullivan" said Agnes, his secretary as the intercom blurted out

"A Colonel Martin is here to see you sir," said Ms. Crumley.

Thank you." replied General Sullivan. as he released his button. the door opened up and walked through.

"You All Remember Capt. Martin. as you can see now Colonel Martin," said General Sullivan.

"General Sir, I'm honored to be called up, so I came as quickly as I could," said Martin.

"General Sullivan!"

"Yes, Agnes" as he pushed the talk button on his intercom.

"A Lt. Colonel Augustus Washington, and master Sgt. John Henry Jefferson, are here for their meeting sir!" said General Sullivan secretary. as the door opened a new wave of handshakes and hugs as if they just seen each other yesterday. and oblivious to the 10 men in the room was a couple sitting in the corner watching 23 to 40 years of friendship all unfold.

"Ladies and Gentlemen," as heads turned? unaware of Doc.

"Crow" said Wilson.

"Which one is he, is it, Leo, Jack, Ray, Harold, Leonard, or Bob. It would be, Leonard!" said General Sullivan.

"Mme. the name is Shea, Decatur Shea!" as he took her hand, kissing it, and then saying.

"You're as pretty as a mess of Yellow Jasmine in the early morning spring dew. I am sure in your father-in-law's ramblings. he has mention my name!" said Shea.

"No sir, not at all?" replied Doc back.

"I've not known General Sullivan that long? we just met!" said Doc.

"And how long have you known, Junior?" said Thug.

"Well, let me think," said Doc.

"We met! Seven-day honeymoon, we came here last night! and now here I am" said Doc.

"Holy moly, if you're 40 years older and not married, I give the punk a run for his money!" said Wilson with a big smile on his face as he gave Doc a kiss on the cheek and shook Curly's hand.

"Congratulations kiddos all the best!" said Wilson.

"All right, all right! enough of the niceties!" said Sullivan.

"We have a ceremony to commence with first?" said General Sullivan. "Gentlemen get squared away! Lt. Colonel Augustus Washington front and center. Please!" Commanded General Sullivan.

"By the authority invested in me! I now promote you to Lt. General Augustus Washington!" said Sullivan as he handed the stars crossed over with a handshake to the newly promoted General.

"I'm very honored and humbled, but I failed to grasp why?" said Washington.

"November 11, 1918, France, Do you remember that? I said one day, I would ask for a favor. Now it's time to pay the piper! I need you and Doc to join together you take the mental side, General O'Keefe, is the physical side, then you two compare notes get these men and women better, it is rather a large step in helping our troops and sailors getting back to recover from war!" said General Sullivan. "Master Sgt. Jefferson. Front and center! You are now being promoted to the rank of Sgt. Major." The General shook Jefferson's hand and put his other hand on top of his shoulder.

"Right ladies and gentlemen listen up! I cannot tell you enough times, we are on the threshold of war! I called you altogether! because you're going to be me staff for the upcoming conflict." stated General Sullivan. as he sits behind his desk, pulling the upper right drawer out! Producing a letter.

"Ladies and gentlemen, I have some bad news that I like to convey to you from a telegram, I just got three days ago, from the old soldiers home," said General Sullivan.

"We regret to inform you that one Lt. General, Clancy Clust O'Rourke, Esq. and Brig. General Aloysius Finn Gilhooly, Esq. quietly passed in their sleep one hour from each other!" said General Sullivan.

"I have in my possession an unopened bottle of Bush Mills! I say we break this open, and toast around to General's Gilhooly and O'Rourke to of the finest officers you'd ever want to serve with," said General Sullivan.

"Boyo, when Crow said they would toast a round, is it a around for you? then around for me? or are the cheap bastards combining the toast," said, an awfully familiar, but now ghostly Irish brogue.

"Clancy, your eye patch is on the wrong, eye? we shouldn't have to wear our eyepatch up here?" said Gilhooly voice.

"True, but who says where up here? by the way, I've earned it, by Saint Michael!" said another familiar voice Irish brogue.

Then again, the men are oblivious to the couple sitting in the corner. Then, Doc says to Curly. "You think we have time to find a fancy place to eat? I'm famished!"

CAST LIST

DOCTORS

Dr. Fredora "Doc" Sullivan	Natalie Portman
Dr. Katie QuinnCannon	Kate Beckinsale
Dr. Hilda von Haag	Diane Kruger
Betty Brown	Scarlett Johansson
Sue Lee	Lucy Liu

NANKING

Dr. Bob Wilson	Woody Harrelson
John Rabe	Jürgen Prochnow
Minnie Vautrin	Mariel Hemingway

MARINES

Bromhead Boone	Chris Hemsworth
Winthorpe Windridge	Tom Hardy
Chris Reynolds	Ryan Reynolds
Tom Hook	Ryan Gosling

CHINA

Old Li	Jackie Chan
Rev Black	Robert Downey Jr.
Valentina Brandt	Olivia Munn
Captain Leonard Sullivan	Chris Pine
General Sullivan	Brendan Gleeson
Mary Magdalene-Waugh Sullivan	Meryl Streep
Major Mugen Mo	Ken Watanabe

WASHINGTON

Stephen Forthright	Chris Evans
Sgt. Major Tom Lightfoot	Rudy Youngblood
Sgt. Major John Lightfoot	Raoul Trujillo
President Roosevelt	Jon Voight
Lt. General Decatur Shea	Tom Hiddleston
Colonel Ronald Smedley	Dan Fogler
Lt. Colonel Augustus Washington	Denzel Washington

A PRAYER FOR TODAY

This is the beginning of a new day. God has given me this day to use as I will. I can waste it---or use it for good, but what I do today is important, because I am exchanging a day of my life for it!

When tomorrow comes, this day will be gone forever, leaving in its place something that I have traded for it. I want it to be gain, and not loss; good, and not for evil; success, and not failure; in order that I shall not regret the price I have paid for it.

—Anonymous